MATADOR, MI AMOR

Borgo Press Books by WILLIAM MALTESE

MATADOR, MI AMOR

A NOVEL OF ROMANCE

WILLIAM MALTESE

"My Love" Romance Series

THE BORGO PRESS

MMXII

MATADOR, MI AMOR

FIRST EDITION

Published by Wildside Press LLC

www.wildsidebooks.com

DEDICATION

For Christine Havens,
Who has joined me on many a
Sunday afternoon for wine and bullfights

CONTENTS

CHAPTER ONE

This was Extremadura, east out of Trujillo, south-west from Madrid and hugging the border with Portugal. Rocky. Its very low hills were burned (often by temperatures over one hundred degrees Fahrenheit) by the Iberian sun to various shades of ochre and tan dotted, here and there, with olive groves.

"It's a man's land," Karen Dunlap had told her daughter. "What Lalo was thinking when he left it to you completely escapes me."

Alyssa's mother hadn't found her daughter's sudden inheritance anything more than a tidy piece of real estate to be quickly dispensed with on the marketplace.

"You go for days on end, out there, without seeing even a bird. Of course, there are the bulls; but, you never really get to see them, either. They're sequestered off in the countryside, miles away from any man, woman, or child, who might approach them on two legs and spoil them for the bullring."

Karen had been at the Montego Hacienda for only one month, twenty years ago: the one and only month she'd been Señora Karen Montego, wife of Spain's chief *matador de toros* Lalo Montego. It was a month and a marriage she didn't care to recall, even now. One about which she still very seldom spoke.

"He had to have been crazy," Karen had decided, "up to the very end. Why else leave the ranch to you when he has a son by that Cartaga Woman."

The Cartaga Woman was Talia (nee Valéndez) Montego; although, Karen never gave her a Christian name. As far as Karen was concerned, Talia was, and always would be, simply the Cartaga Woman: Lalo Montego's first and third wife. Talia had preceded, and, then, succeeded Karen in Lalo's bedroom. The logical explanation was that Lalo had married Karen on the rebound and had had second thoughts when he was given the opportunity to get Talia back. After all, Talia had given Lalo a son, Adriano; and, in the end, she was the only one of Lalo's six wives (seven marriages) who did. His mistake in marrying Karen became evident when, still on their honeymoon, he had engaged in a sexual relationship with a married lady on an adjoining ranchero. It was that affair which had sent Karen so quickly to divorce court.

Alyssa wasn't Lalo Montego's daughter. Her father was Donald Dunlap, Boston socialite, married to Karen for less than two years when he was shot dead in the crossfire of police and three bank robbers.

Immediately thereafter, Karen had pretty much abandoned her daughter to a series of nannies, tutors, and private schools, to become an instant member of the international jet set and "café society", picking up three more husbands in the bargain, one of whom had been Lalo Montego.

Then, after her last divorce (this time from a Swiss banker), Karen had decided to settle down; although, she had long since passed the point of ever really seeming like a "mother" to her daughter, neither having seen much of each other over the years.

Alyssa had met only two of her mother's four husbands, counting her father. And, Lalo Montego hadn't been one of them. That Alyssa had been made primary beneficiary of Lalo Montego's Spanish estate, quite a sizable holding, left her more than a little bewildered.

"Turn it over to all over to lawyers," Karen had counseled. "Let them sort it out with Adriano's lawyers, because Adriano won't stand by and see you get his birthright without a fight."

But when the lawyers suggested the property be liquidated, Alyssa decided, quite on impulse, that she wanted to see it first.

"It's no place for a woman," Karen had persisted. "Take it from someone who has been there, done that, got the T-shirt, burned it, and tossed the ashes. You'll feel completely cut off from civilization."

If she'd been more attuned to her daughter, Karen would have realized that it was just that kind of escape for which Alyssa was looking, needing somewhere to where she could escape and re-think her decision to break up with Ty Gordman.

Everyone, her mother included, was sure Alyssa had slipped off the deep end the minute she not only refused Ty's proposal for marriage but stopped seeing him altogether. Not only was he handsome, but his family connections made him one of the better catches among the always surprisingly few prime bachelors available.

Certainly, Alyssa "liked" Ty. But, liking and loving, at least as far as she was concerned, were not one and the same. She enjoyed his company, because he was polite, well-mannered, danced well, made pleasant conversation, and could make her laugh, but that didn't mean she enjoyed him so much as to contemplate spending the rest of her life with him.

Alyssa was enough of a romantic to envision marriage as the beginning to an eventual "death do us part" ending. On the other side of the same coin, she was enough of a realist to see that, perhaps, such long-lasting marriages were not usually the rule. Where divorce had once been looked upon as an anathema by the rich, it was now a course of action even they embraced at the drop of a hat.

The driver, Flavio, said something, calling Alyssa from her reverie and back to the present. He was pointing.

Ramón Selene, seated in the seat beside Alyssa, immediately scooted forward for a better look at circling birds in a patch of cloudless blue sky off to one side.

Ramón was the foreman of the ranch Alyssa now owned. He'd met her at the airport in Madrid. They had been driving since morning, except for a short break for lunch.

Never very talkative with his new employer, perhaps logically made ill at ease by the presence of a young American woman who probably didn't know a bull from a heifer, he had lapsed into complete silence long before the car passed through Toledo en route to Trujillo. He wasn't silent now, though, even if his animated conversation was with the driver and not with Alyssa.

The birds, obviously the subject of conversation, continued their downward helix over something probably dead.

"...go for days without seeing even a bird," Karen had said. But, surely, a few buzzards shouldn't be cause for such excitement.

Alyssa strained to catch segments of the conversation. After all, she did speak the language, forced into it by obligatory foreign language lessons heaped upon her by a long line of tutors and teachers in private schools. But as she had discovered in France, on her first visit, there was usually a period of transition needed, wherein it was necessary to recognize the language spoken by the natives wasn't the same sterile language taught in classrooms far removed from the countries in question. Flavio and Ramón were simply speaking too fast for her to translate.

The car came to a sudden stop. Ramón opened his door and got out.

Alyssa realized there were several horsemen approaching from one side. Once abreast of Ramón, who was standing beside the car, the horses stopped. Ramón talked several minutes with the riders before getting back into the car.

"Is something wrong?" Alyssa asked as he again joined her. The riders were reigning for a turn-back the way they'd come.

"Some difficulty," Ramón admitted, obviously reluctant to continue with an explanation. He wished she weren't around to ask questions. He would have undoubtedly been more at ease if—whatever the present problem—he were able to handle it himself, without having the new owner right there to look over his shoulder.

"Whatever it is, I'm sure you can handle it," she said, deciding she really wasn't up to pretending she could even begin to be in charge of the situation. She had come here to escape and think, not become involved in playing enthusiastically at ranching. "I've been informed that you continue to do an excellent job in overseeing the property."

If she had assumed her ready delegation of authority would relieve her of the problem, she was sadly mistaken. As much as Ramón might have preferred relieving her of it, there was no way he would be able to keep any of this from her if she decided to stick around for any length of time.

"Another bull has been killed," he said finally.

Flavio put the car into gear, and they again started moving.

"*Another* bull? *Killed?*" Her curiosity was aroused in spite of herself. "Some disease killed them, you mean?"

"No," he admitted reluctantly. "Some*one* killed them. With a gun."

"A gun? Some *one*? For heaven's sake, how many did this someone kill?"

"We've found four."

Outside, there wasn't a cloud (only buzzards) in the sky. Shimmering bands of heat lifted from the plain. Dust rose with the heat, stirred by God only knew what, since there was hardly a breath of breeze to be had anywhere. Trees, whenever making their occasional appearance, were either the gnarled limbs and trunks of olive, or some other low, squat trees which Alyssa wasn't able to identify. The latter had dull silver trunks and twisted branches that extended to all sides. She couldn't help being reminded of pain-distorted souls stretching arms upward for relief from Hell's blast-furnace heat.

Karen had been right when she described the landscape as "more suited to a man's tastes". It definitely lacked the slightest feminine touch—at least at this point in Alyssa's observations of it.

"Who?" she asked. "I mean, any suspects? After all, who goes around shooting helpless animals?"

"Yes, who?" Ramón echoed, though he, unlike Alyssa, had his suspicions. "Whoever, we'll find him. The ranch is large, but nowhere is it so big as to hide a person like that forever. That I promise you."

Why did Alyssa shiver? How could she chill in heat so long having penetrated the car, despite the air-conditioner on at full blast? Was it something to do with the revelation that, somewhere, out there, was someone with a gun, who might decide humans were worthier targets than stupid, four-legged beasts?

Or, was she letting her imagination run rampant? Certainly, Ramón had never said anything to insinuate that whoever killed the bulls might soon be looking for two-legged victims. Possibly, it wasn't all that big of a deal after all. Despite vast economic improvements, Spain still had a moneyed elite and an extensive population of poor; one of the latter possibly just found him or her brought to the point of killing for....

"Food?" she suggested. It was more than apparent, by the look Ramón gave her, that he hadn't been anywhere near following her mental conjecture. She hurried to clarify. "The bulls, I mean. Did someone, perhaps, kill them for food?"

"Oh," he responded, finally getting the gist. "No."

So, Alyssa left it at that, hoping he would be able to take care of it after all. Frankly, she couldn't imagine what difference a bull or two made in the long run. She had seen the figures that indicated the presence of over a thousand of them on the Montego Hacienda.

Once again, the conversation jolted to a complete stop. Alyssa pushed herself back into the leather seat and dreamed of arriving at the ranch where she could, hopefully, surrender herself to the unadulterated luxury of a long bath.

At least a dozen more miles were eaten up by the speeding car, and Alyssa began to wonder if she was ever going to see a bathtub before nightfall. She still had no real concept of the size of the ranch she'd inherited and found it hard to register how it had been well over an hour since Ramón had indicated they'd just passed over the eastern edge of her property.

Finally, the car turned right into a lane that bisected a grove of olives. The trees betrayed their age by displaying gaping holes that often formed tunnels from one side of a tree trunk to the other. A novice would have insisted such trees had likely seen their last days. However, the trees' full canopies of delicate leaves, silvery-gray on the bottom and dark green on top, parenthesizing clusters of small black fruit, proclaimed otherwise.

After the barrenness of the land through which she'd just driven, Alyssa found this bit of visible green decidedly refreshing.

The grove gave way to a coppice of old and impressive oaks, attractive as only those particular trees can somehow be. Suddenly, in amongst them appeared the first evidence of well-manicured lawn, and—yes—water spurting rhythmically from a sprinkler system. Alyssa's dreams of a bath were suddenly resurrected.

The hacienda sat amongst more oak, olive, and fruit trees. It was a large house, in the Spanish style, with white-washed adobe and red brick, the latter echoing the ferrous content of the soil in the area. The windows, large and overhung by balconies, were lined with lattices of iron grillwork seemingly so insubstantially delicate as to remind Alyssa of a lace mantilla she'd seen in the duty-free shop at the airport in Madrid.

Also, suddenly, there were flowers, complete carpets and tapestry-like cascades of them, gold and red, blue and white, able to survive within the parameters of this small oasis where they would quickly have perished beyond the availability of life-giving water.

When the car door opened, and Alyssa stepped out, the first thing she smelled was how the perfumes, exuded by the many blossoms, hung so heavily— almost palatably—within the air.

"Flavio will see to your things," Ramón informed, giving Alyssa immediate leave to precede him up the three steps to the entranceway leading to the main door of the hacienda. The whole access area was embraced by a cupping grape arbor that's intricate weave of vines and wood supports dangled delectable clusters of green grapes and dappled the sunlight.

One of two massive panels, each inset with its own polished bronze bull-head whose metal nose ring acted as a door knocker, came open. Before Ramón could introduce the emerging, heavy-set woman to the new mistress of the house, though, a commotion erupted somewhere around a corner of the building, out of sight.

Ramón glanced at Alyssa, his look one of my-God-what-can-possibly-be-happening-now-?

"Mara!" he yelled, by way of instructing the plump

woman just through the door that Alyssa Dunlap was now fully in her charge, with or without formal introductions. He was quickly off and running to find the cause of the to-do.

"Viene...viene!" Mara insisted, coming to shoo Alyssa into the house, much like a mother hen moved to protect her brood from a fox in the hen house.

Alyssa complied, but only because she couldn't imagine doing anything else. Certainly, she wasn't yet confident enough in her new position to insist on following Ramón to the source of the continued confusion that sounded very much like men fighting.

What was going on, here?

If she were expecting answers from Mara, she was disappointed.

"What's happening?" she asked finally, having yet to discover that Mara's realm was the house, and anything beyond its walls was usually of no concern of hers.

"Men!" Mara said, by way of all-encompassing summation and flashed a wide and welcoming smile.

"Fighting?" Alyssa asked, uncertain whether she asked a question or made a statement. It made no difference, since Mara paid no mind, on either account.

"I'll show you to your room," the portly woman said instead. Her English was good, albeit with a decidedly sing-song cadence that seemed almost Oriental. "We'll get you a nice bath, and I'll bet you're ready for some fresh clothes, now, aren't you?"

"Indeed," Alyssa admitted. Since she doubted any access to the continuing brawl outside, even if she wanted it, which she didn't, she decided to let it run its course. If Mara wasn't concerned, why should Alyssa be? Most likely, Mara's insinuation that men were simply men was apropos for even this particular occasion.

"This way," Mara instructed and led the way through a large living room and up a wide flight of stairs.

The second floor had rooms that opened up from a balcony that overlooked the living room. Alyssa's suite offered access to a second balcony that overlooked the inner courtyard of the hacienda.

"Beautiful!" she exclaimed, looking down on the tranquil loveliness of palm trees, cacti, flower beds, well-trimmed shrubs, geometric walkways, benches, and a central splashing fountain. For the first time, Alyssa had some comprehension of just how truly large the hacienda was.

"*Sí, muy hermosa,*" Mara admitted before disappearing into the bathroom. There was the inviting sound of hot and cold water blasting to mingle within a white-porcelain tub.

There was as rap on the door, and Alyssa moved automatically to open it. Mara beat her to the punch, though, emerging from the bathroom with surprising speed. Alyssa wondered at the keen sense of hearing which had allowed Mara to hear the knock over the bath water.

The opened door revealed a young boy, probably in his early teens. He had a head of dark curly hair, dark black eyes, and clear, dark-complexion. He was dressed all in white, except for his sandals, which were made of twisted yellow hemp fiber. He carried a wood-and-tile tray on which was a frosted silver pitcher of liquid, a glass, and a plate tented by a linen napkin,

Mara plucked off the napkin, critically eyeing the arrangement of small sandwiches she'd uncovered. When everything under her scrutiny apparently passed her inspection, she silently nodded the youth her permission for him to enter the room and place the tray on one of the available small tables. His job complete, he beat a hasty retreat, punctuated by a shy smile when Alyssa, for a brief moment, managed to catch his eye.

"Something light to eat," Mara said, "and some lemonade, from freshly squeezed lemons, to hold you over until later." She poured the latter.

"Yes, please" Alyssa accepted the glass, appreciating its coolness against her fingers and palm. Although a slight breeze somehow managed to enter over the balcony, the heat of the progressing afternoon, out-of-doors, was still evident within the room.

"Fresh lemonade, a bite to eat, a nice bath, followed by a brief siesta, and you'll be feeling yourself, again, in no time," Mara promised, as if she were a doctor prescribing the ultimate cure. "You'll see."

"Yes," Alyssa said, more than ready to agree. She found it enjoyable to be in the company of this friendly servant, more so than with the obviously ill-at-ease Ramón. At least, Alyssa had sensed intuitively Ramón had been made ill-at-ease—likely by her. She knew just enough about Spain to suspect its men were still so steeped in their false illusions of "macho" as not to appreciate being placed completely under a woman's authority.

Why had Lalo Montego, Spain's most macho of macho, left his bulls and his estate to Alyssa, instead of to, Adriano, his own son? No one had yet been able to answer that question to Alyssa's satisfaction—and certainly not to the satisfaction of her mother.

"Lalo always was screwing up his loyalties," Karen had said to her daughter. "But, then, he ever only professed to have had but one true friend: Joaquín Hidalgo. And, he showed just what he really thought of that, didn't he?"

As much as Alyssa had pressed for more details, Karen hadn't obliged.

"Best not stir up that cesspool at the moment," had been her mother's concluding comment.

Alyssa now placed her glass back on the tray, picked up one of the remaining sandwiches and followed Mara into the bathroom.

As Mara helped Alyssa out of her clothes, Alyssa took stock of herself in the un-steamed segments of the mirror. She decided, as she always did when she took the time for cool analysis of herself, that she was neither all that good nor all that bad in the looks department.

Actually, she was being modest, as any man would have gladly told her, had he but been given the chance. Alyssa had spent a good deal of her life behind mansion walls, and within all-girl schools, relatively sheltered from men and their compliments.

Actually, Ty Gordman had been the only real boyfriend she'd ever had. Although he told her often enough that she was beautiful, she wasn't prone to believe him, especially since he was so obviously too smitten to be truly candid.

"Where else, my dear, do you plan to find another man so handsome, so socially well-connected, and so head-over-heels in love with you?" Karen had frankly wanted to know.

Alyssa had been tempted to ask just what made her mother any great authority on what did, or didn't, constitute a good marriage prospect, since none of Karen's marriages had turned out any great success story. Often, Alyssa found herself wondering if even her mother's marriage to Alyssa's father would have survived if forced to stand the real test of time.

Mara's eyes were less critical than were Alyssa's of the young woman's obvious charms. Mara knew a real beauty when she saw one and could appreciate that Alyssa had somehow managed to arrive at young womanhood without being obnoxiously aware of her physical perfection. Mara had seen more than her share of attractive young women paraded through that very house by Lalo Montego when he was alive. The majority of those great beauties had been so aware of their physical attributes that their knowledge had made them less appealing than they might otherwise have been.

"Is the water too hot?" Mara asked, watching Alyssa tentatively begin her descent into it.

Actually, the "tub" was a small pool built into the floor, lined with the same sunburst-centered deep blue tiles that covered the walls, floor, and ceiling.

"The water's fine," Alyssa answered, taking one more small step down into the glaze of steaming liquid heaped, here and there, with fluffy mounds of bubble-bath-spawned suds.

In the mirror, her duplicate reflected back: blonde hair, smooth skin, exquisitely long legs, slim waist, ample breasts, and sensuous shoulders and neck.

She sat, letting the water cover all of her except her

neck and face, as Mara moved quickly to pile Alyssa's mane of hair atop the young woman's head and wrap it securely into place with a heavy towel.

Mara, who only vaguely remembered Alyssa's mother, was quite convinced Alyssa could lay claim to most of the mother's remembered good looks. That said, from what Mara could divine, on such short notice, the daughter's disposition was far better than the mother's had ever been. Then, again, Lalo Montego had something about him that eventually made all of his women less than lovable. There had been something decidedly destructive about Lalo's relationships with women— and men. Any woman. Any man, except, maybe, for Joaquín Hidalgo. Mara conjectured that Lalo had never loved any of them. All he had ever loved, up until his bitter end, had been his precious bulls and the times he spent in the *corridas* with them. At least Alyssa had been spared Lalo Montego.

Lalo had been the victim of a bull-horn thrust which should never have caught him in the belly. He'd been way too old to be fighting bulls in the bullring at the time. Yet, he couldn't stay away; and, despite what some people had thought, it had nothing whatsoever to do with the large sum of money the promoters had paid him for his come-back. Lalo Montego always had plenty of money, even before he ever stepped into his first bullring as a boy of thirteen.

For some reason, he had simply been drawn to the *corrida*, even at the very end. Apparently, it had made no difference that his coordination wasn't what it had once been, nor that the bulls were no the less dangerous.

No matter what all the bleeding liberals said, the bulls were not always destined to be bested on every Sunday afternoon. Ask Lalo Montego, wherever he was—in heaven or, more than likely, in hell.

Kneeling to wash Alyssa's back, Mara didn't like to think of Lalo actually in hell; although it was suspicions of his presence there that saw her praying for his soul each and every night. He had destroyed and mangled a lot of lives, even if he had always been kind to her. But, then, he had never really loved her. If he had, she, too, might have come to have a different impression of him. Strangely, it was the ones Lalo seemed to love the most (if he loved at all), who had ended up suffering the most at this hands.

"Do you think it would be all right if I just stayed where I am for awhile and just soak?" Alyssa asked, knowing that Mara had finished on her back and was now merely going through the motions. "It really feels so glorious."

"You soak, then," Mara said. "I'll go unpack your things to makes sure it gets done properly. As you'll soon find out, some of the girls around here need someone to take a firm hand. I've tried my best to keep them in tow; but, any great house needs a master or mistress in residence to take up the slack resulting from most everyone's natural inclination toward laziness at the first opportunity."

"You'll have to help me, Mara," Alyssa said. "Until I get the rhythm of things, I'm afraid I'm rather out of my element."

"Don't you worry, honey," Mara told her. "You'll do just fine."

The servant retreated to the other room where Flavio had unobtrusively deposited Alyssa's luggage.

Alyssa slipped deeper into the womb-like warmth of the water. She laid her head against the edge of the tub and shut her eyes. She didn't actually fall asleep; but, she was very close to it when Mara returned to yank a large Turkish towel from the warming rack.

"You don't want to stay in there so long as to catch a chill," Mara warned with concerned authority.

Reluctantly, Alyssa obeyed her summons from the bathtub, enjoying the warm towel that quickly wrapped her.

The bed was turned down, revealing its crisp white sheets and providing a welcome invitation, indeed. Alyssa, whose last couple of days seemed filled with plane and car rides, suspected she was beginning to suffer the nemesis of all long-distance travelers: jet lag.

"What you need now is siesta," Mara informed.

"After which, you'll be in good shape."

Alyssa exchanged the towel for one of her night-gowns and crawled into the bed.

She must have gone to sleep as soon as she hit the mattress. Though, it didn't seem all that long before she was being coaxed back to consciousness by a gentle but insistent nudge of her arm.

Pulled drapes had converted the room into twilight; even though, it was still daylight outside.

Alyssa stretched deliciously, enjoying the sensuous pull of her muscles and spine. She recognized Mara by the bed. She didn't notice the concern etched on the Spanish woman's face.

"Oh, but that did feel good," Alyssa said. She added, somewhat guiltily, "I could have slept for hours."

"I'm sorry to have disturbed you, *Señorita,*" Mara apologized, but...."

"No apologies necessary," Alyssa interrupted, threw back the lone sheet which covered her, and came to a sitting position. Her toes sought out, and found, the slippers that Mara had put beneath the bed earlier. "Certainly, I didn't come all of this way to spend all of my time in bed."

Her slippers on, she stood and snatched her robe from the back of the nearby chair. She walked to the windows to throw back the drapes and let in sunshine which, somehow, seemed less hostile than it had during her long drive to get there.

It was only when she turned back to Mara that she realized the Spanish woman was concerned about something.

"Whatever is the matter?" Alyssa asked, moving closer to Mara. Now, there was no mistaking the anxiety written in the expression on Mara's matronly face.

"Ramón wanted to see you, whenever was convenient," Mara informed. "I told him you were sleeping; but he now insists that what he has to say really won't wait."

And, that sounded more than a little ominous!

"Do you know what he wants?" Alyssa asked. At the same time, she wondered what she should wear, until she realized Mara had already solved that problem by having laid out a white blouse and a light blue skirt.

Mara answered by delivering an exaggerated shrug.

Alyssa suspected the woman knew what Ramón wanted but probably wasn't talking. Alyssa contemplated giving her the third-degree, but, then, rejected that as being out of hand. Whatever it was Ramón had to tell her, she would find out soon enough.

"Tell Ramón I'll be down shortly," Alyssa said.

"I did keep telling him you were still resting," Mara mumbled under her breath as she exited the bedroom and pulled the door shut behind her.

Alyssa hurriedly dressed and spent a quick few minutes at the vanity table getting her hair and face back into presentable shape. Then, she left the bedroom and headed along the hallway to the stairs that descended to the living room.

Ramón was standing, not sitting, as if he were uncomfortable inside the big house and would have far preferred sitting a horse somewhere out on the plain.

"Ramón?" Alyssa greeted as soon as he'd spotted her. "Mara said you have something urgent to tell me."

"Urgent, yes," he agreed. He held his hat in both hands, twisting it along its brim.

"Would you like to sit down?" she suggested.

He shook his head, obviously wanting none of that.

She waited while he continued to say nothing and look extremely ill at ease.

"There's a problem?" she ventured, thinking that the way things were going, the two could very well end up standing there all night.

"The bulls," Ramón said finally.

Alyssa decided he was quite charming in his nervousness. He was probably younger than she originally suspected. The sun had a capacity for aging people beyond their actual years.

He had shiny black hair that looked as if it would soon need trimming. He had large black eyes, full mouth. His nose looked as if it might have been broken once—even twice; the slight misalignment, though, didn't detract from his overall good looks.

Consciously, she brought her mind back to whatever the problem at hand. It certainly wasn't the time to be appraising the help's physical attractiveness.

"What about the bulls, Ramón?" She wondered how he could be persuaded to just come out with whatever it was he had to say. She was beginning to fear that she might have to extract the information piece by piece, like a dentist pulling a cracked tooth.

"The dead bulls," he obliged, finally, before stammering to yet another silence.

"The bulls that were shot...by someone, you mean?"

"Yes," he affirmed.

"Why don't you simply tell me what you have to say, Ramón?" she suggested, trying to be patient. "At this rate, we're liable to be spending this day and the next rooted to this very spot."

"The men," he said, paused, and then continued, "brought in somebody. He's out in the barn."

"Brought in whom? Out in what barn?"

"They were angry," he explained cryptically. "Understandable, yes?"

"I see," she said, really not sure she was seeing anything at all but hopeful she was making progress of sorts. Eventually, the pieces of the jigsaw were bound to fall into place.

"It's the son," Ramón said so lowly that Alyssa almost missed what he said.

"The son?" she jumped in on the faintly delivered cue. "Whose son?"

"*Señor* Montego's—Adriano."

"Lalo Montego's son, Adriano? Where?"

"Out in the barn."

"He's the someone who has been killing my bulls?"

"I think you should come," Ramón said. "The men are upset. You understand."

"Certainly, I understand," she said, knowing intuitively that, come what may, it was an owner's position to take the side of employees. Why was Adriano Montego killing her bulls with a gun? And, what was he doing back here, now, in that he had dropped out of sight during the time period in which the will was going through probate, surprising Alyssa's mother to no end when he hadn't protested the delivery of the Spanish property into her daughter's hands? The way Alyssa came to understand it, Adriano would have had every reason to be upset by the share his father had left him, compared to what was left a young woman Adriano had neither met nor seen. For some reason, Lalo and his son were on the outs at the time the elder Montego met his death in the afternoon.

"If you think I should see him, then, of course, I shall see him," she said. "As a matter of fact, why don't you take me to him now?"

"Yes," he agreed, obviously relieved. Had he actually assumed that she, as a woman, would break down and become hysterical?

They headed for the door where Mara magically appeared with a scarf for Alyssa's head.

"You don't want to get sunstroke your first day here," Mara said.

Alyssa thanked her and followed Ramón outside, around the house, and off toward the stables and the barn in the distance.

She looked for indications of her other employees and saw none. It seemed strange that, since her arrival, she had seen only four people: Ramón, the foreman; Flavio, the chauffeur; Mara; and, the young boy who had delivered the tray of sandwiches and lemonade to her bedroom.

After all, the ranch had a permanent payroll of over one-hundred people. And, while some of those undoubtedly spent most of their time out on the range, watching the bulls, some of them had to be in charge of upkeep at the hacienda and its immediate grounds. Possibly, the regulars from around the house were just staying low, waiting to see how Alyssa was going to cope.

"Luís!" Ramón called.

Alyssa realized her initial surveillance of the emptiness had failed to pick out one man partially shielded by a couple bales of hay. He left his spot and headed in their direction. He had been so positioned as to have Alyssa wonder if he'd been strategically placed to keep people out of the barn, or to keep one particular person in.

Ramón made perfunctory introductions. Luís looked uneasy, almost to the point of embarrassment. Alyssa kept her greeting to a slight nod of her head in his direction.

"Quiet?" Ramón asked Luís.

"*Sí,*" Luís replied.

"Good." Ramón continued forward, drawing Alyssa and Luís in his wake. He stopped beside the barn door and turned to Alyssa.

"They were angry with him, you understand?"

"I don't care who he is," she said. "He shouldn't have been killing my bulls, should he?"

"Exactly," Ramón agreed, hopefully beginning to realize that his new boss did understand, even if she was a woman easily misconstrued to be less likely to comprehend things like loyalty to the land, and to the bulls, and....

"Shall we go in and see Mr. Montego, then?" she suggested. She was curious to meet the son to whom Lalo Montego had left so little.

They entered the shadows of the barn. It took her

several seconds to adjust her vision to where she could even make out shadows within shadows.

The place smelled as only a barn could smell: a not totally unpleasant mingling of hay and straw, of animal and animal dung. There were no animals in immediate evidence, though. Alyssa assumed the horses were kept in the separate stable complex. Whatever animals lived here on a permanent basis (cows?), were obviously now out to pasture.

"Over here," Ramón guided.

She wasn't sure of her coordination in strange surroundings and followed slowly. Luís took up the rear.

Ramón led the way to a far stall. At first, Alyssa couldn't see Adriano Montego at all.

"My God!" she exclaimed when she finally *did* see him curled up in a battered ball on a compressed pile of hay against the wall.

Ramón and Luís exchanged nervous glances of which Alyssa was intuitively aware.

"But, then, if he was killing bulls, he undoubtedly deserves his present condition, doesn't he?" she ventured in an attempt to put Ramón and Luís more at ease. In actuality, she wasn't at all sure that killing a few dumb animals should have really warranted beating Adriano quite so badly. "Still, I suppose the most humane thing would be to get him a doctor." She turned to Ramón. "Wouldn't you agree?"

"Of course," he said. The last thing he wanted was a dead Adriano Montego in the hacienda barn.

"You know of a doctor who would be discreet?" Alyssa continued, trying to assuage whatever her foreman's continuing obvious fears. She had knelt by Adriano's body, afraid he was already dead. Her immediate fears had been somewhat lessened by the pulse evident at the base of his throat seen without her even having to touch it.

"Luís, go get Leandro!" Ramón commanded. He turned to Alyssa and explained, "Leandro isn't a real doctor, but he knows enough to tell us if we'll need Dr. Santos from town."

Alyssa wasn't at all sure she was willing to risk Adriano's diagnosis to someone medically unqualified. Still, she had asked for someone discreet, hadn't she? She didn't want trouble to come from this, if it could, in any way, be prevented.

"Mr. Montego can't stay here," she said, thinking of very little else to say under the circumstances. Luís had already left the barn, en route to fetch Leandro— wherever it was Leandro might be that he hadn't been summoned already. "Shall we take him to a bedroom in the house?"

"I think it would be best to wait," Ramón said. He didn't know how badly Adriano was hurt, but he didn't want to take any chance of making him worse by moving him. If only he had gotten back to the hacienda earlier, he might well have stopped things from having gone this far.

Damn—Adriano should have known he was playing with dynamite when he killed those bulls! If he knew nothing else, he had to know how these men idolized those animals. Bulls were these men's lives. To kill one of the bulls, let alone five of them, before even one of them could meet its natural end amid the pomp and circumstance of the *corrida de toros,* was sacrilege. Adriano Montego was lucky he wasn't dead. He might well have been if Ramón hadn't arrived when he did.

"Yes, of course, you're right. We mustn't move him," Alyssa said, wondering whatever had possessed her even to suggest doing so. How many first-aid courses had she taken in her life wherein it had constantly been drilled into her as to just how dangerous it could be to move any victim before qualified medical help arrived on the scene?

CHAPTER TWO

Leandro Galba turned out to be the local self-trained veterinarian. That made Alyssa, when she found out, a little uneasy. The general consensus of Ramón and Luís seemed to be that they would trust the diagnosis any day of a man who handled the bulls, over the diagnosis of Doctor Santos from town.

Alyssa became even more worried when Leandro pronounced his verdict of Adriano Montego's condition: "Actually, he looks a whole lot worse than he really is."

Alyssa was sure that had to be wrong. As far as she was concerned, no one could possibly look like Adriano now did and not have broken bones, internal injuries, or both.

"What I prescribe is plenty of bed rest somewhere a bit more conducive to comfort than this barn."

"It's all right to move him, then?" Alyssa asked, anxious for verification that the veterinarian had, indeed, said Adriano was likely to remain among the living.

"Oh, it's quite safe to move him," Leandro assured. Then, seeming to sense Alyssa was dubious, he added: "Of course, if you would prefer to call in a second opinion, I'm sure Dr. Santos in...."

"I see no reason for a second opinion," she said, trying to pretend that idea hadn't even crossed her mind.

"Well, if you find he's not improved by tomorrow...." Leandro let the sentence purposely hang, insinuating by doing so that Alyssa could still summon Dr. Santos if she wanted.

That had all taken place over twenty-four hours ago. If Adriano Montego hadn't yet regained consciousness, at least he was looking better.

Alyssa, who had momentarily taken the chair beside his bed, took another opportunity to give him the once-over. She felt her cheeks grow hot as she remembered how she'd been so reluctant to leave the room when Mara had begun undressing him for bed.

"You'll want to step on out, for a minute, my dear," Mara had instructed Alyssa, upon realizing the younger woman hadn't been any too quick to make an exit. "I'll take care that the young man is properly made ready for bed; not something to be attended by a proper young lady like you."

Alyssa had wanted to stay, even though she had been embarrassed when caught trying. She told herself her desire to stay had been nothing more than natural curiosity. What else could it have been, since Adriano had hardly looked like God's gift to women with his swollen eyes and split lip? Besides, Alyssa had never seen a naked man. Not in the living flesh anyway. There had been a couple of nude scenes in movies, but those just weren't the same thing.

She wondered how many women, at twenty-six, still hadn't seen an on-the-spot naked man. She wondered how many hadn't gone a bit farther than just the seeing. There had been a few times in her life when she'd been tempted to step over the boundaries of innocence and arrive on the next plateau. She had been kept from it solely because she hadn't had all that many opportunities. Despite the rumors, girls' schools weren't the best places to get practical experience in the facts of life. Not the private schools she had been cloistered within, anyway. The one located closest to a boys' academy had been the one she had attended in Switzerland. The boys, though, had been across the lake; and, the faculties of both schools had, by the time Alyssa arrived, long since learned every possible ploy their charges might come up with to get together. Those same faculties had known how to run expert interference.

As for Ty...well...he had tried a couple of times to get fresh, but he had been easily put off. After all, he'd been brought up to respect women of Alyssa's ilk and to vent his animal lusts elsewhere. Quite frankly, though, Alyssa had always suspected he was much too genteel to have animal lusts. Admittedly, she was just as genteel, but she imagined her lusts smoldering just beneath the surface, just waiting for some special man to come along and fan them into full-fledged flames.

Those thoughts made her blush redder. She was back daydreaming something she used to, a good deal of the time, when younger. What young woman didn't dream of her knight on horseback? It was quite all right and healthy for a young girl to fantasize such things. On the other hand, it was hardly all right for healthy twenty-six year old woman to continue harboring such flights of erotic fantasy.

The focus of her attention went back to the man on the bed. If her mental computations were correct, she figured he was about two years her senior. The swelling and discoloration on his battered face had gone down far enough to show that he was a recogniz-able twenty-eight—and attractive as hell, if you liked dark, brooding, good looks on a man.

He had black hair, fairly short but pleasantly tousled to hang a curtain of confused strands over his fore-head. He had black eyebrows that almost, but not quite, came together. His eyelashes were long and lush, resting on his cheeks now that his eyes were shut. His mouth showed indication of being full and sensuous even without the additional bee-stung look caused by his split lower lip. He had a decidedly square jaw that managed to escape being overly blockish with its deep chin-cleft so deep as to leave Alyssa wondering how he possibly shaved within its inner crease. And, he obviously was a man who had to shave regularly or show the effects. Since the time she'd brought him from the barn, his face had grown noticeable stubble. The hair on his arms and along the visible top of his chest grew atop an intricate display of well-delineated muscles.

Something told her it might be interesting to see how the men who had beaten him had fared. It seemed unlikely that a man in Adriano's superb physical condition would have stood idly by while pounded senseless.

He groaned; in direct response, she scooted closer to him and the bed.

He rocked from side to side but not enough to change his supine position. Finally, the rolling stopped.

He opened his mouth, licked his lips, and twisted his face into a grimace when his tongue slid over his injured lip. His eyes fluttered, then opened, revealing large, ebony pupils that immediately seemed to suck Alyssa into their depths.

"Where am I?" he asked.

Alyssa smiled. She had heard that trite line so often in movies that she had come to suspect no one would actually ever use it in reality. "Resting, in that I'm afraid several of my men became a bit overwrought when they discovered you were shooting my bulls and decided to use you as a punching bag."

"Stupid fools!"

"Granted, they may have overreacted just a bit, but I'm a little loath to criticize them too thoroughly since they were responding to the destruction of my property, weren't they?"

"Except that I didn't kill your damned bull!" His dark glance nailed her to her chair as firmly as a stick pin pinioned a bug to corkboard.

"I suppose there are always two sides to any story," she said, magnanimously. She didn't want him to think she was automatically accepting his tale over the one told by the men who worked for her. Though, she couldn't imagine Ramón a liar, and he had said the men had done what they had done because Adriano Montego had killed another bull. "Why don't you tell me *your* side of the story?"

"I was on my way to make a courtesy call on you, as it happens," he said. "I heard a shot. I rode over to find the dead bull. Your men appeared and jumped to false conclusions, then jumped me."

"Well, you must understand how they might well have come to the conclusion they did, right? I mean, the circumstantial evidence against you must be obvious, even to you."

"Even though I wasn't carrying a gun of any kind at the time?" he challenged. His effort at sarcasm curled his lips and obviously caused him pain.

"No gun?"

"Your bull was strangled to death, was he?"

Just because he wasn't found with a weapon didn't mean he hadn't had one. Hearing the approach of the riders, he might well have found someplace to hide the weapon he'd used for the distasteful deed. Despite the temptation to confront her uninvited guest with that ready possibility, Alyssa didn't do so. Since Ramón wasn't there to hear her confront Adriano, she decided, momentarily, to give Adriano the benefit of a doubt.

"If that, indeed, turns out to be the case, I'll owe you an apology," was all she'd concede at the moment.

"Why? I didn't see you laying into me with your pretty fists."

"Yes, but my men were acting on my behalf," she reminded.

"And, did your men do much damage? If it's as much as it feels like, I must be in sad condition, indeed."

"Actually, as I understand it, your wounds are superficial, if decidedly painful at the moment."

"Says Dr. Santos?"

"Well...," Alyssa began and then stopped. She wondered how she would confess that she had turned him over to a veterinarian. "In truth, I was so afraid you might be seriously injured that I had to look closer to home than Dr. Santos."

"That would mean Leandro Galba? Yes?"

She was about to launch into how she had been assured of Leandro Galba's qualifications, when Adriano surprised her.

"Actually, I've long had my suspicions that Leandro is the better of those two doctors," he said. He tried smiling but failed because of the pain that the stretching caused his battered lips.

Alyssa was relieved. It gave her something to quote if he ever decided to bring any of this into a court of law. She didn't know how the courts moved in Spain on cases of assault and battery, but she suspected a judge and jury might be a little concerned about anyone who called in a veterinarian rather than a qualified doctor. But, if the victim admitted to the veterinarian's expertise, well, then....

"Do you suppose I could have some water" he asked, interrupting her train of thought.

She reached for the pitcher and glass which Mara had put by the bed earlier. She tipped the pitcher, filled the glass with water, and handed the result to Adriano.

He sipped, managing—if with a good deal of difficulty—to get the glass emptied and passed back to her.

"Am I causing you a major inconvenience by being here?" he asked, slipping deeper between the sheets.

The heaviness of his eyelids disclosed that he was tiring quickly.

"The hacienda has enough spare bedrooms so that I don't think I'll soon be pressed to remove you from this one," she said, deriving a sudden satisfaction from her role of Florence Nightingale.

"Nine of them, as a matter of fact," he said, managing a faint grin. "Bedrooms, I mean. My father, your benefactor, managed to use each and every one of them."

Alyssa wasn't really all that sure of a proper response to that—if there even was one. As it turned out, any response would have been superfluous, since Adriano drifted suddenly into sleep.

Alyssa sat for a few moments more by his bedside, wondering how much his facial features would be altered once all of the swelling was down and his split lower lip mended.

Once again, she made mental comment as to how Adriano Montego was one attractive man. She got up and left the room, closing the door behind her.

In the hallway, she passed two young girls, both of whom were loaded down with linen. Over the preceding few hours, most of the servants had begun to resurface from the woodwork into which they'd seemingly disappeared. Alyssa acknowledged the girls with a nod of her head, determined she would eventually have to gather all of the household staff for a more formal introduction once she was more settled in.

Then, again, maybe not. It wasn't as if she was planning to stick around, was it? It wasn't as if her knowing, or not knowing these people was of any great importance. If she sold the property, as her mother advised her to do, it was probably best if she didn't get close to any of them.

She was halfway down the stairs when she heard the knock on the front door. Mara, as usual, managed to materialize out of nowhere to answer it.

"Mara, how are you?" the man, still outside, said by way of friendly greeting. He was an older gentleman, quite distinguished in demeanor.

"The *Señorita* Dunlap is upstairs," Mara said. "If you would like to come inside while I go get her...."

"Mara?" Alyssa called to her.

Mara turned, as did the man parenthesized by the doorway.

"Is it someone for me?" Alyssa asked. She couldn't imagine what kind of business the man could have with her.

"*Señor* Joaquín Hidalgo to see you, *Señorita*," Mara informed.

"*Señorita* Dunlap?" he queried. "I'm one of your neighbors and hope I haven't chosen an inopportune moment to stop by."

"You say your name is Hidalgo?" Alyssa wondered

why his name rang inner bells. The idea that she actually knew him, or even some distant relative of his, seemed highly unlikely.

"Joaquín, please," he insisted. "I was driving by and thought I'd stop to welcome you. If it's an inconvenience, however...."

"Of course not, *Señor* Hidalgo...."

"Joaquín, please," he, again, requested.

Suddenly, Alyssa remembered. In the flesh and blood, here was the one man her mother had insinuated was once Lalo Montego's only true friend. *Once* had been the key word, in that Karen had, also, insinuated that Lalo had done something quite dastardly to destroy the friendship; although she'd never been persuaded to go into any detail.

So, what was he doing there, now? Had he really only stopped on a neighborly visit?

"Won't you come on through to the courtyard, Joaquín?" Alyssa invited.

Simultaneously, she wondered how many Spanish taboos she was about to break. She had read all of those stories about how unmarried women in Spain never entertained gentlemen without *duennas* in attendance. Surely none of that archaic formality, though, could possibly apply to Alyssa. It seemed absurd that she might somehow assume that it did. She was an American, and, thus, definitely removed from Spanish mores. Also, she was owner of the hacienda. That surely removed her from the necessity of any chaperones, even if she had been Spanish.

That Joaquín had arrived in the expensive Mercedes sports car parked outside, and not by horseback, was evident by his exceptionally neat appearance. He wore a white turtleneck sweater, blue blazer, and pressed, complete with creases, dark blue pants.

Alyssa led him to a table in the courtyard and motioned for him to sit.

He was dark-complexioned, had black eyes, gray-streaked black hair, sensuous lips, and what looked like a very good body. Alyssa found the total package decidedly handsome.

"Would you like a drink, *Señor*...Joaquín?" she asked.

"If it wouldn't be too much bother, perhaps some wine?" He smiled pleasantly.

"Of course." She glanced to Mara who took her cue, turned, and left for the kitchen.

"Once again, I hope this visit isn't an inconvenience," he said, eyeing Alyssa with the appreciation of someone who had obviously had enough contact with women to enjoy the company of an attractive one when he happened upon one.

"Not at all." She wished she'd thought to tell Mara to bring two glasses. "It's nice to know one's neighbors.

You say you live nearby?"

She was hard-pressed to figure out where any immediate neighbors could possibly live. Unlike in the States, where they were usually just down the block, or a few miles away, at most, here she had the definite impression that she could drive for hours through nothing but her own property.

"Off in that direction," he said, motioning toward the north. "The original settlers, perhaps sensing the isolation so easily afforded by owning such large tracts of land, conveniently built haciendas within commuting distance of adjoining points of properties. There's my ranch. Yours. And, that of Victoro Isidro. All joined together like three massive pieces of one giant pie. In fact, one purpose of my stopping by was to see whether or not you would be inclined to attend a small get-together I'm holding this weekend. It's nothing overly fancy, you understand. I'm expecting a rather important matador as my houseguest. He's agreed to test some of my heifers for bravery. It could prove decidedly entertaining, and it would give you an excellent opportunity to meet more of the locals."

Mara appeared and carried a tray that—Alyssa was pleased to see—sat two glasses of red wine. Mara delivered Alyssa's glass first, and then Joaquín's, before leaving.

Joaquín sampled his wine, flashed Alyssa another

dazzling smile, and complimented her on her wine cellar.

Alyssa was quite content to have this handsome man in attendance, no matter what his motives in coming. While she had come to Spain seeking rest and relaxation, a time to just sit and think, she couldn't help admitting she rather enjoyed the idea of attending a local get-together to see some "rather important" matador fight heifers. It was the kind of exotic invitation usually received only in the movies, not in real life.

"You will come?" he asked after another sip of his wine and another smile.

"This weekend?"

"Saturday. Come early. Around ten. Usually, I like to start out with a large breakfast, followed by a light lunch, then siestas before turning everyone loose at the *corrida*. I could even send a car for you; that is if Adriano hasn't beaten me to the punch."

"Adriano?" It was an automatic response that, had she had the time to think about it, she would have never made. She'd given the false impression she hadn't the foggiest notion who Adriano might be, when, in fact, the man was in one of the hacienda bedrooms at the top of the stairs.

"Adriano Montego," Joaquín said, seeming somewhat surprised that she had responded as she did. "I believe he's your stepbrother—or was at one time."

"Of course," she admitted. "I don't know what I was thinking."

Knowing that Joaquín knew Adriano somehow made Alyssa extremely nervous, even if, since Joaquín had once been Lalo Montego's best friend, it seemed logical that Joaquín and Adriano would know each other.

"He did stop by yesterday, didn't he?" Joaquín asked. "He said that was his intention."

"Actually...," Alyssa began and then hesitated. She'd been on the verge of telling a lie, even so far as denying she'd seen Adriano at all. Before she could get that out, however, she contemplated the possible repercussions. Lying now was liable to cause all sorts of difficulties later. What possible motive could she give for denying everything now, especially if she wanted to come out of this as the wronged party? It seemed unavoidable that word of Adriano getting beaten up by her men was eventually going to get out. Too many people were involved to keep it any big secret for long. Her denying everything, now, would solve nothing, and, likely, raise all sorts of embarrassing conjecture at some later date.

Obviously made curious by her pause, Joaquín still managed to wait for her to reply in her own time.

"This, I'm afraid, is a little awkward," she said finally, deciding to begin again. "I presume Adriano

Montego and you are friends."

"As was his father and I," Joaquín said.

She found that confusing. From the inflection of his voice, it might well have been assumed that he and Lalo had been friends up until the very end. However, Karen had insinuated quite differently. So, what kind of game was Joaquín Hidalgo playing, or had Karen got it wrong?

"Adriano could well be a good friend of yours, too, if given half the chance," Joaquín said. "I can personally vouch that he holds absolutely no animosity toward you because his father bypassed him to leave you the ranch. In fact, I think he was rather relieved. He's the exception to the general stereotype that has all Spaniards revere the bulls. Actually, Adriano can't stand them."

"Can't stand them?" she queried for clarification.

"Probably because his father was so determined that Adriano follow in his footsteps," Joaquín said. "I feel quite confident that had Adriano been left on his own, without having had *el toro* rammed down his throat, morning, noon, and night, he would have probably taken a far more favorable outlook on *la fiesta brava.*"

"Just because he didn't like the bulls wouldn't mean that he would...well...kill them, would it?"

"Kill them?" Joaquín's full lips spread into another smile. He had even white teeth. "Adriano's father would have given anything to see him take to the ring and kill more bulls. The truth is that Lalo was furious whenever his son refused to do so. Adriano, you know, would have made one hell of a matador. Heaven only knows, he certainly had at his disposal the very best tutors to illustrate proper technique. However, he seldom fought real bulls, only the mock-ups used for practice."

"I didn't mean kill them in the bullring," she said, wondering how she was going to come across without sounding ridiculous to Adriano's friend. "I meant kill them with a gun."

"A gun?" Joaquín response seemed genuine surprise. "I'm afraid I'm not following."

Alyssa took a larger swallow of her wine than she intended. She thought for a quick moment she was going to choke and thanked God when she didn't.

"Yes, a gun," she managed finally.

"I'm afraid I still don't understand."

"Actually, my own understanding of what has happened isn't the best, I assure you," she confessed. "You understand that I did just arrive yesterday afternoon, completely ignorant of anything except that this ranch had been left me by Lalo Montego? I've since come to understand that several of my bulls have been...killed...shot."

"My God! And you suspect Adriano?" His tone indicated he surely must have imagined any such insinuation.

"Unfortunately, your friend was found standing over a recently killed bull yesterday by some men from this ranch."

"Surely not!" Joaquín swallowed the last of his wine and set his empty glass to one side.

"I'm afraid the sight of him, standing over the dead animal, was...well...for my men...a bit disconcerting."

"I should think so," he said, obviously not needing her to go into any additional details in order for him to get the picture she painted. "Is Adriano all right?"

"The doctor assures me that it's only superficial wounds, but Adriano does *look* pretty bad."

"Dr. Santos saw him?"

Alyssa paused, once again faced with the embarrassment of telling someone she had agreed to call in a mere veterinarian to oversee Adriano's condition. What would Joaquín think?

"He looked so bad, I'm afraid I rather panicked and sent for someone a bit nearer than Dr. Santos," she admitted finally.

His expression told her that he expected something more specific.

"A man...." She found it so hard to admit it had been a veterinarian. "...by the name of Galba."

"Leandro Galba?"

"You know him?"

"He's probably a better doctor than Santos," Joaquín said: one more person putting Alyssa's guilt to rest. "But, don't ever tell Santos that if you ever see him, will you? He gets a little upset if anyone suggests medicine can be learned purely by on-the-job training."

Alyssa smiled, more as an expression of relief that from genuine amusement.

"Can I see him?" he asked.

She thought for a moment he meant "see" Leandro Galba. Quickly, she recovered, however, to realize he had to mean Adriano.

"Certainly, we can look in on him," she said. "He was sleeping, though, a few minutes ago."

She came to her feet and led the way.

At first, Adriano did appear to be asleep; so much so that Joaquín told Alyssa they wouldn't disturb him. However, at the sound of Joaquín's voice, Adriano's eyelids fluttered and opened.

"We were about to call in the mortician to carry you away," Joaquín said, addressing the conscious Adriano. He went over to the bed and stood by it. "My friend, you do indeed look like hell! Whatever in the world happened?"

"A mistake," Adriano said, licking his lips.

Sensing that he wanted a sip of water, Joaquín reached for the nearby glass, filled it with water, and handed it over.

"Obviously, a mistake," Joaquín echoed. "Thank God, I'm informed that you're not nearly as bad as you look; so, count your blessings."

"You will, I hope, verify to *Señorita* Dunlap that I'm actually a quite respectable character?" Adriano ventured. If he couldn't smile, his eyes were at least capable of twinkling amusement.

Alyssa marveled how he could retain even a trace of humor, and wondered if she would have had any remaining if she'd been beaten unconscious.

"I've already told her as much," Joaquín assured. "I think she might even believe me."

Alyssa was glad that neither man turned to her for verification. She wasn't prepared to make any commitment at this point. As owner of the ranch, with a responsibility to the people who worked for her, she wasn't about to admit her men had been in the wrong until she was positive they had been—maybe not even then. The sudden revelation by Joaquín that Adriano hated bulls had only enforced her suspicions that Adriano might not be as innocent as the two men would like her to believe.

"Does the good doctor say you'll be up and around for my fiesta this weekend?" Joaquín asked.

Adriano handed back the glass. "And, if I'm not there, no big deal, yes?" He did sound as if he really wasn't all that interested in witnessing the planned testing of heifers for bravery by some matador.

"Of course, it would be a great loss!" Joaquín argued, "Fanuco has his heart set on making a good impression on the son of Spain's once most illustrious matador."

"Fanuco," said Adriano, with a coolness that surprised Alyssa, "is an insecure fool!"

CHAPTER THREE

The cook, who Alyssa had just discovered was as very good one, had prepared *sopa de guisantes, ensalada de pepinos,* and *cordero lechal asada.*

Alyssa forked the last piece of the juicy roast lamb that remained on her plate and eyed Adriano through the candlelight flickering between them. Over the past three days, most of the swelling in his face had gone down. The discoloration had faded to where it was hardly noticeable against his naturally dark complexion.

In the attractive lighting, she couldn't even discern the bruised and battered man she had discovered in the barn a few days before. For that matter, having become more and more acquainted with her houseguest, she couldn't quite believe he could have taken a gun to any of those bulls which had been found dead.

On that same account, Ramón had recently admitted, albeit privately to Alyssa, that the ranch hands had, perhaps, acted a little too spontaneously since a thorough search of the locale where Adriano had been discovered revealed no concealed weapon.

"If it was a mistake, it was a natural one, to be sure," she had told Ramón. "You tell the men that I'm quite prepared to stand behind them in what they did." This she said to impress Ramón, since Alyssa was pretty sure he had doubts as to whether he should even have informed her of the continuing absence of any incriminating gun.

As far as Adriano was concerned, Alyssa thought it best not to mention how the search for the weapon had turned up nothing. She didn't want to give him any ammunition, just in case he should still decide to make some kind of legal fuss. Not that he had indicated he had any such plans. Quite to the contrary, he had magnanimously stated, at one point during his recovery period, that he might well have jumped to the same faulty conclusions had he stumbled upon someone standing over a newly slain bull.

"I think the men are more in control now," he had said after Alyssa had found he had left his bed one morning to stroll the grounds. "Actually, I had quite a peasant walk without being set upon by even one of your employees."

Yes, time had done wonders to repair the damage done during the fisticuffs. He looked even more handsome than ever. Alyssa couldn't help but be somewhat affected by the decidedly romantic qualities of the evening in progress. Not that she was romantically inclined toward Adriano, or he toward her. Heavens, but that would have been carrying her illusion way too far! But, she had always been susceptible to the notion that candlelight, good food, excellent wine, and an exceptionally handsome man were all the ingredients from which good romance was made. If she didn't love Adriano, then there was certainly no harm in at least relaxing enough to enjoy the moment, and, perhaps, spice it up with a bit of harmless flirting.

"Delicious meal, delicious company," he said. His slight smile revealed an attractive dimpling of his left cheek.

"Wait until you taste dessert," she said. "I've been assured it's the cook's specialty."

"Ah, that would be Destina's renown flan," he said. "It is, indeed, a treat for which to look forward."

And, Alyssa was shocked back to the reality that, of course, he would know that the cook was known for her caramel custard. After all, Adriano had eaten it how many times in his life? This hacienda had been his home for most of his life, hadn't it? If anyone was the stranger here, it was Alyssa, not he. Traces of his residency still remained on the premises, even without the man's physical presence. He had some of his things packed away in the attic. His clothes still hung in several of the closets. In fact, what he was now wearing had been produced from one such closet to replace what had been torn and dirtied beyond repair during his beating.

"Suddenly, you seem a million miles away," he observed, bringing Alyssa's meandering thoughts back into focus on the reality before her.

"Yes, I suppose I was," she admitted, without bothering to go into any detail. Simultaneously, she wondered how she would have felt had Lalo Montego been her father and left the family estate to a complete stranger. Wouldn't she have harbored some kind of resentment toward the interloper? "You must forgive me. I'm afraid I still have to pinch myself occasionally to bring home the fact that I'm in Spain, sitting at a table with the son of Spain's illustrious Lalo Montego."

Adriano smiled, his dimple concaving more deeply than before. He had a very pleasant smile that only made his handsome features even more striking.

"Where are you staying?" she asked. "I mean, I know you're staying here, at the moment, but you weren't anywhere in residence when I arrived."

"No," he admitted. "Somehow, I thought you might be ill at ease to find me here. I took a few of my things over to Joaquín's. He's kindly agreed to put me up until I can decide where to go from there."

"I'm a little confused about Joaquín Hidalgo," she said, hoping finally to get that little mystery cleared up.

"How so?"

"I understood your father and he had a falling out."

"Dad and Joaquín?" He made it sound ludicrous.

"You mean, they didn't?"

"Not as far as I know. Where did you hear that they did?"

"From my mother."

"Hmm." Adriano shook his head in apparent confusion. "I can't imagine how she came to that conclusion. Certainly, Dad and Joaquín maintained a chummy relationship all of the time I was around. Dad was saying up until the very day he died, that Joaquín was the one person he had hoped never to hurt. They grew up together, you know?"

"Maybe my mother got her wires crossed," Alyssa suggested. "It wouldn't be the first time."

Adriano looked as if he were giving the subject additional thought.

"Although, I never could quite figure out why he was against...." He let the sentence hang as if genuinely sorry he had shifted the conversation.

"Against what?" she pressed.

"Ladonna's engagement," he admitted finally.

"Ladonna?"

"Ladonna Hidalgo. Joaquín's daughter."

"Your father was against her engagement?" She was more curious than ever.

"I wouldn't quote me on that." He gave a nervous little laugh. "Dad never did come right out and say as much. It was just a feeling I eventually came around to having at the time. Even if true, it could hardly have had anything to bear on this supposed blowup to which your mother referred, could it?"

If it had no bearing on anything, she wondered what had made him bring it up. Diplomatically, though, she chose to take their conversation elsewhere.

"As I said, my mother probably heard something and then blew it all out of proportion."

"Most likely that's what happened," he said, by now ready to prescribe to that particular theory.

"So, back we go to your present living situation. Do you plan to stay on at Joaquín's indefinitely?"

"That's rather a good question, I suppose. Actually, I haven't really made any definite long-term decisions beyond the point where I am right now. I figure I haven't abused Joaquín's hospitality to such a point, yet, that he's on the verge of kicking me out on my rear. That's one advantage to having him as such an old family friend. Besides, you needn't really be concerned, if that happens to be the reason for you asking. My father didn't actually leave me destitute, you know. He had to leave me something for fear I would rush off to the law courts and try to make his will worth little more than the paper on which it was written."

"Frankly, my mother expected you to do just that," Alyssa said candidly. "Tie up the estate in lengthy litigation, I mean."

"That's because the older one gets, the more one becomes obsessed with money, property, and possessions," he said. "Had I been older, like your mother, I might well have fought the will. But, twenty-eight isn't all that old. And, in the end, I'm quite convinced that I would rather go out and make my own way in the world than be shackled with the world my father managed to erect before he died."

"You aren't resentful, then, that he left the hacienda and the bulls to a stranger?" Now that she'd finally broached this line of conversation, she was reluctant to abandon it.

However, there was the lull necessitated by a young man suddenly there to replace their plates and another young man to serve up delicate molds of caramel custard. Finally, there was a new bottle of white wine needing to be uncorked to go with the dessert.

"I'm not at all resentful," Adriano immediately picked up the conversation once Alyssa and he were again alone in the large dining room bordered by its four walls hung with the portraits of...Adriano's ancestors?...men and women, many of them on horseback. "And, besides, you're no longer a stranger, are you?"

Alyssa blushed. Adriano was—and, for not the

first time—taken in by the young American woman's attractiveness. If the candlelight and the atmosphere muted what remained of Adriano's cuts and bruises, it also worked to emphasize all of Alyssa's many good points. Her hair seemed exceptionally golden, her eyes exceptionally purple, her mouth exceptionally inviting, and her neck exceptionally graceful.

"You could stay here, you know," she suggested, wondering what she was thinking. "I mean, of course, until you decide just what you planned to do with yourself."

"I'm not at all sure that would be the best thing for your reputation," he replied.

Alyssa looked for his smile of amusement and found it. "I'm not sure I follow you," she said, although she knew she was lying. For some reason, she found the idea of having him around a very inviting one. Without him, she was surrounded only by servants and ranch hands. On the other side of the same coin, she hadn't come all of this way for a social life, rather for seclusion, peace, and quiet.

"How would it look if you, a single young woman, had me, a single young man, living in the same house?" he ventured, leaning forward. His voice had dropped into a lower, conspiratorial octave, and there was a definite edge of amusement playing throughout it.

"Granted, I'm inclined to believe people everywhere

are prone to grab at the first opportunity to gossip" she admitted, leaning toward him—although, there continued to be a wide length of table separating them. "But, you and I are almost brother and sister. I mean, when you come right down to the bottom line, we can correctly argue that we're *still* stepbrother and step-sister. Yes? Since when, then, is it so scandalous for relatives to live together under the same roof?"

"Since I hardly look upon you as my stepsister." His voice got even lower when he added, "In fact, the very idea of someone as attractive as you being related is a bit disconcerting."

That really made Alyssa blush, because, if she wasn't mistaking, he was definitely flirting with her, telling her that he far preferred her in the role of American stranger than even tentatively connected to him by the marriages of his promiscuous father.

"I've embarrassed you," he said, sitting back in his chair and acting—albeit only slightly—apologetic. "But, surely you must realize how attractive you are. Yes? And I, after all, am only human, and a man to boot. While I, undoubtedly, do have many faults, one of them is not the inability to appreciate a pretty face and body."

Probably what Alyssa found the most embarrassing at that moment was how she hadn't, for a second, looked on Adriano as a stepbrother. That connection between them was so tenuous as to be virtually nonexistent. And, she had found him attractive. She had made her offer, because she wanted to keep him around, if just because, after Ty Gordman, Adriano Montego seemed horribly exciting, exotic, and even dangerous.

It all boiled down, she decided, to her being embroiled in a bunch of romantic poppycock of her own making. Quickly, she determined she was undoubtedly making far too much out of Adriano's little confession. The chances were more than good that he was simply throwing out harmless conversational flattery, much as any young man might do in payment for hospitality rendered by his hostess.

"I'm sure I could survive the gossip if you could," she stammered finally. Was he viewing her as an amusing, naive goose? "So, you might just remember that the offer was made and add it to your list of possibilities." She lifted a spoon and used it to slice off a delectable chunk of the caramel custard which she immediately fed her mouth as a good excuse for not saying anything more for the moment. "Besides," she finally managed between succeeding spoonfuls, "I'm sure the place could use a man's touch to keep things running smoothly. I'm afraid I know absolutely nothing about raising bulls."

"I think you would possibly be far better off to let Ramón take care of the bulls," Adriano said, his eyes downcast and apparently focused on the shimmering mound of molten dessert. "My attitude in the past has hardly ingratiated me to your employees. And, considering recent happenings...."

He let the sentence hang, glanced up, and delivered an expression that seemed just as embarrassed as anything Alyssa had managed to come up with until then.

"Certainly, I wasn't insinuating that you would have to work for your keep," she said, rushing to fill a silence she felt was in the making. "You're welcome to stay on, whatever the circumstances."

"I appreciate your offer of continued hospitality," he said, deciding to leave any decisions until later. He had to admit the idea was tempting. Also, he had to admit that he found Alyssa Dunlap, perhaps, a little *too* tempting. While he had been less than completely serious when he had pointed out the possibilities of scandal inherent in his remaining at the hacienda beyond the point of his complete recovery, and while he was nowhere nearly as promiscuous as his father had been, he certainly wasn't beyond feeling certain basic instincts spawned by a man's confrontation with a beguiling female. He decided he would have to do some in-depth analysis of his feelings toward her before he made any kind of commitment to live under the same roof with her. For, if one thing among all the others was a certainty, it was that he never had thought, and probably never would think, of this ravishing young woman as his stepsister.

"This is delicious custard, isn't it?" she said after searching for a neutral area of conversation that would relieve the tension. There was, indeed, tension in the room. Although it certainly couldn't be identified as entirely negative, its presence did somehow managed to quicken the flow of blood through Alyssa's veins, making her physically excited. She felt charged with electricity; as if by reaching out she might send an arc of sparks flying in any direction.

"Destina is known far and wide for her flan," he said, echoing what Mara had told Alyssa earlier. "It's rumored that people used to come from miles around on the pretext of visiting my father just to sample the dishes his cook put on the table."

Alyssa realized she hadn't even known the cook's name before Adriano mentioned it. Really, it was unforgivable on her part, except that she had decided not to form any kind of ties, here, hadn't she? She had utilized every imaginable excuse to keep away from more personal contact with the staff. Still, even if she were only planning a stay of a few weeks—or, at most, a few months—it seemed unbearably snobbish that she should go about her business, pretending real people, with names, and lives, were nothing more than inanimate objects whose sole purpose was to provide for her comfort.

Take the meal in question. It had been delicious, prepared with obvious care and skill by a woman whose name Alyssa hadn't even known until a few seconds ago. Destina was obviously more than a short-order cook. It was about time that Alyssa got beyond the point of treating her like one.

"Let's call Destina in and thank her, shall we?" she suggested. "Do you think she'd be offended?"

"Offended?" Adriano provided an accompanying laugh. "Destina lives for her cooking. She's happiest when she knows it's enjoyed."

"She's probably delighted, then, to have you back to eating," Alyssa said. "I'm afraid that up until tonight I haven't been ordering things much of a challenge to anyone's culinary skills."

As if sensing she was wanted—servants long in-service somehow are able to develop a feel for such things—Mara made her appearance. Alyssa asked to see the cook for a few minutes if the woman was available.

Destina looked like a cook who thoroughly enjoyed her own cooking. She was a large woman, even more so than Mara. She had apprenticed in this very kitchen under the cook who had supervised under Lalo Montego's father. By the time Lalo had taken over control of the estate, Destina was more than prepared to handle the scheduling of dinners, parties, and fiestas that had accompanied Lalo whenever the great matador had finished a season of the bulls and had returned to his ranch. She was just as skilled at preparing the intimate suppers for two that had been required even more often than banquets for hundreds.

The woman, though, was exceedingly nervous when she was informed the new mistress of the hacienda had asked to see her in the dining room. Since Lalo's death, Destina had about decided she might retire from service. The ranch just wasn't the same without the hustle and bustle that had surrounded Lalo's fame in the *corrida*. She had taken momentary hope, what with the arrival of Alyssa Dunlap, that the good times might somehow be resurrected, but that hope had immediately paled when the attractive young American showed no indication whatsoever of becoming the hostess Destina had hoped she would become. In fact, until word had been passed down that Alyssa wished something a little extra special to be prepared for that evening, it seemed the young woman was content to survive on nothing but cold chicken sandwiches.

Destina had expected to be summoned long before this and had been somewhat curious as to why she hadn't been. Mara kept insisting that it would take the American woman time to get settled, but Destina knew that if the new owner didn't establish her authority in the household soon, she would have difficulty ever doing it.

Destina was exceptionally surprised that Alyssa had called her to the dining room not to put forth some sort of criticism but actually to compliment on a job well done. And, if for a second she suspected it had been Adriano who had put her up to it—Destina had always liked the young man, even if his manliness had so often been put into question because of his reluctance to face the bulls—that suspicion was soon laid to rest.

"I would have suggested accolades myself," Adriano told Destina, "but Alyssa beat me to the punch."

Destina certainly didn't overlook the fact that Adriano had progressed beyond calling the mistress of the hacienda by her last name.

"I'm afraid I've been a little lax in my duties," Alyssa said, flashing a friendly smile that had Destina thinking the young woman just might be capable of taking control after all. "I'll stop by sometime tomorrow for a longer talk."

"You've almost got her completely in your corner," Adriano announced when Destina had exited the room flushed with pride. "Now, if you just assure her you will be doing quite a bit of entertaining in the days to come, you'll have her licking out of your hand. Destina is always at her best when there is the prospect of a few hundred critical palates waiting in the wings to be satiated."

"Unfortunately, I'm hardly in any position to entertain," Alyssa said.

The custard dishes had been cleared away. The wine had been replaced by large snifters of cognac.

Alyssa swirled the liquid inside her bulb-like liqueur glass. She wondered if she should inform Adriano of her intention of selling the estate.

"Certainly, it can't be a question of facilities or finances," Adriano observed. He was well acquainted with the cash settlement, quite aside from the ranch, bestowed on Alyssa by his father.

"It's a question of acquaintances," she answered. "So far, the only two people I even know, hereabouts, aside from some members of the staff, are you and Joaquín Hidalgo."

"Ah, but after Saturday's *tienta,* you will have countless acquaintances to draw from for your guest list," he said with an expansive wave of his hands.

"Tienta?"

"A testing of animals for bravery," he defined, though Alyssa's Spanish had so remarkably improved since her arrival that she was actually able to catch the gist of most words, no matter how quickly they were spoken. "Are you a fan of the *corrida,* Alyssa?"

She hesitated in making a reply, because she knew Adriano apparently looked upon the bullfight with a good deal of aversion.

"Joaquín is thoroughly caught up in *la fiesta brava,* and he and I have managed to remain good friends," Adriano informed, obviously sensing the route her thoughts had taken.

"In truth, my exposure to bullfighting has been very limited," she quickly confessed. "It's not your everyday American sport, you know."

"Actually, it's not considered a sport at all, in Spain, but an art form," he corrected.

"So, there you see how much about it I really know," she said with a shrug that laid her case to rest. "I've seen only one *corrida* in my whole life. That was in Tijuana, Mexico. I was twelve at the time. My mother was dating a Commander in the U.S. Navy, and he was stationed in San Diego. We all left after the third bull, my mother insisting all the scheduled matadors were novices. I think, although she never did indicate any real fondness for the art form, that she had, by then, as now, still come to think of herself an authority, having at one time been married to your father for a whole month."

Adriano grinned. Having never met his father's second wife, he had always wondered just what Karen had been like. She would have had to be a good-looker, or Adriano's father wouldn't have bothered. And, of course, Alyssa's beauty gave clear indication of the genes on her mother's side of the family.

"So, whether I'm a fan or not, at this point in my life, is up for grabs," she admitted. "I do remember my mother assuring me that the bulls died far more humanely in the ring than in the slaughterhouse. Also, I do remember how they're bred to do what they do, so I mustn't assume they're helpless domesticated animals turned loose for mere butchering. 'A domestic bull,' my mother informed me, 'would run like hell at the first placement of a *pic*, let alone still be charging after the *banderillas*'."

"Your mother undoubtedly did her homework." He lifted his cognac to his nose and sniffed before swallowing some of it.

"You don't agree as to the spectacle being more of a religious ritual than anything else?"

"Certainly, it's a reenactment of life," Adriano said, "and of death."

There was a pause of uneasy silence, wherein Alyssa tried to think of something to say. It was Adriano who ended up filling the void.

"You may be surprised to learn," he said, "that I'm not actually against the *corrida,* per se. Actually, I think Spain would be far less the Spain that I love if there were no bullfights."

"But, I thought...."

"Yes, I know what you and a helluva lot of other

people thought and think," he interrupted. "But, you've, now, the benefit of getting it directly from the horse's mouth. What I have against bulls, you see, is that they are big, and they are dangerous. And, that at my very first *corrida,* a big *Concha y Sierra* bull called Borbón gored my father and put him in the hospital for two months. Quite frankly, that scared me to death. It's as simple as that: I hate them because I fear them. However, I don't hate or fear them to the point where I would ever consider gunning them down when they couldn't fight back."

Evidently, he suspected Alyssa of still harboring some doubts as to his innocence in the killing of her bulls—gun or no gun found.

In the same instance, his admission of being capable of fear somehow brought him all that much closer to Alyssa, in that the young woman found that admission of his vulnerability exceptionally appealing. She found it a decided strength that he was able to admit to his fear. Most men, her fiancé included, would have gone around pretending that nothing whatsoever on God's green earth could possibly faze them. The importance of "macho" certainly wasn't a posturing exclusive to Spaniards. Every man she had ever known—at least up until now—had displayed a certain me-Tarzan-you-Jane mentality, at one time or another, which she had always resented.

"Anyway, let me thank you for the delightful dinner and companionship," he said, coming to his feet. "I don't want to play the party-pooper, but, if I'm going to look fit as a fiddle for the fiesta this Saturday, I'm afraid I really must call it a night."

"You'll think about staying on here at the hacienda?" She was surer than ever that she would like to have him around.

"We'll both sleep on it," he said, coming around the table to pull out her chair.

She stood and turned to find she was standing close—very close—to him. She didn't pull back, either, and, neither did he.

They were so close that she could make out the slight discoloration that still lingered along his left cheek-bone. She could see the faint line of mended skin on his lower lip and wondered if there would be a permanent scar.

He smelled of fresh lime and pine trees.

She felt heady and suspected she possibly had drunk too much wine and too much cognac. She reminded herself that she couldn't allow herself to get carried away by the nearness and the attractiveness of this handsome man. Yet, it was difficult for her to keep her rational thoughts separated from her fantasies, especially when he took her in his arms and pulled her even closer to him.

She felt the muscles of his chest and stomach. She felt the way his strong arms encased her within them. She saw his eyes with their large pupils that seemed hypnotically to draw her deeper and deeper into them.

She tasted the flavor of him when he pressed his mouth against hers and forced her lips open with insistent pressure. He tasted of mint and cognac: a flavor that lingered long after he had released her mouth, released her body, and stepped away.

"You see the complications that would arise were I to move back in here?" he told her in a husky whisper before he turned and left the room.

Alyssa reached for the tabletop in order to steady herself. She was sure she had to be dreaming. It had to be merely a combination of the wine and cognac, the candlelight and her make-believe. It was simply impossible that Adriano Montego had actually held her close and actually kissed her.

Yet, the taste of mint and cognac continued to linger on her tongue, and the smell of lime and pine trees lingered in the air; no mental gymnastics, insisting those were nonexistent, could make them go away.

CHAPTER FOUR

Alyssa sat at the vanity table giving her makeup its finishing touches. That completed, she carefully eyed her reflection, looking for anything in her face that might announce the difference. She felt there *was* a difference, whether she could see it or not. Putting a definition to that difference, however, was easier said than done.

Love? Was that this mysterious something? She had thought that thought before, during the last forty-eight hours, and she had rejected it as out of hand. Although she did, likewise, at this moment of inner reflection, find it was hard to deny. Certainly, the suspicion remained.

Perhaps, it would have been easier had she ever been in love before. Then, she would have had a basis for comparison. But she'd never loved. Not really. Anyway, not in quite the same way she kept coming back to thinking she might be in love now. Oh, she loved her mother, and she loved the memory of her father (although there was really no genuine memories of Donald Dunlap).

What about Ty? Surely, she wouldn't have become engaged to a man she hadn't loved. On the other hand, she had sensed from the beginning of that relationship that there had been something missing in it. Else why had she broken off the engagement and fled all the way to Spain to think things over?

She could admit that it hadn't been love she felt for Ty; yet, it was difficult to admit there was even the possibility she was feeling love for Adriano Montego. Adriano was still a stranger, even if he had been in the house for almost a week. How was it possible for her to be in love with a man who had entered her life so recently and under such unusual circumstances?

"You are imagining things, Alyssa," she told herself, running a finger along her right cheekbone to disturb a bit of makeup that had been perfect as it stood. "Love at first sight isn't something that really happens, no matter how many times you read about it, no matter how many times it's portrayed as reality in the movies. Certainly, it isn't conjured by a few kisses."

"And, there had been a few. Not just the one stolen after their supper together a few nights back, either. Last night in the garden smelling of flowers, he had kissed her again...and again...and again. What's more, she had wanted him to kiss her, had wanted him to continue.

She ran the fingers of her right hand through her mane of blonde hair and shivered slightly at the remembrance of just how it had been to have Adriano's lips working against her own. Adriano's tongue....

She scooted back the bench and came to her feet, telling herself she had to get hold, or she was going to make a fool of herself.

She was affected by the fairy-tale quality of the whole incident: Alyssa Dunlap in Spain; a wounded man on her doorstep; a couple of candle-light dinners; a walk in the garden; a few kisses. It all added up to an interlude, albeit pleasant, but an interlude, nevertheless. The idea that Adriano felt any more toward her than he would have for any other woman under similar circumstances was doubtful, no matter what he might have insinuated otherwise.

She decided she had to look at all of this in the sophisticated perspective with which Adriano was obviously expecting her to view it. People born to money were always seeking new amusements with new people. If she had been left out of the whirl up until now, that merely meant she was the exception to the rule. The best thing she could do for herself was to realize that Adriano and she were embarked upon a harmless flirtation. To hold it up as anything more than that was liable to cause a series of unpleasant scenes and hurt feelings when it all began to grind to a halt. And it would eventually grind to a halt, wouldn't it? Still, it would have been nice if it all....

She was thankful when the knock on the door kept her mind from flying off on another track of pure wishful thinking.

"Yes?"

Mara opened the door.

"*Señor* Montego is waiting downstairs," Mara said.

"Tell him I'll be down shortly." Alyssa reached for a light sweater. Although the days remained uncomfortably hot, the evenings often still, somehow, managed a slight chill; she wasn't really sure how long this soiree at Joaquín's hacienda was going to last, but there was a good chance she would be returning to her own ranch well after nightfall.

She left her bedroom, following the same path Mara had taken before her.

Adriano was waiting at the bottom of the stairs, wearing the same kind of suit she always saw Spanish men wearing in movies: an Andalusian cowboy costume, complete with short jacket, flat-brimmed hat, and spurs. Mostly in black, he looked very handsome. Alyssa was on the verge of telling him so when he beat her to the punch with a compliment of his own.

"You're looking exceptionally beautiful, *Señorita* Dunlap." He smiled. His white teeth and tan went well with the dark material of his clothing.

"Keep up the flattery," she said, feeling in exceptional spirits. Her good humor was, in part, due to his continued cheerful attitude. She had been a little uneasy about the proposed outing at the hacienda of Joaquín Hidalgo, because it revolved around the visit of the young matador, Fanuco de Galena, and Alyssa knew that Adriano wasn't overly fond of the *corrida*. Yet, if he was uneasy about the day ahead of them, he wasn't giving any visible indication.

"It wasn't flattery, by the way," he said, leading her to the door and opening it.

"Quit while you're ahead," she said with a laugh that couldn't hide the fact she enjoyed the compliments, no matter what she said.

They drove to the Hacienda Hidalgo in one of the sports cars that was stored in the garage.

"We could have gone on horseback," Adriano said, and grinned amusement. "But if you haven't ridden for awhile, you might have arrived a little too sore to enjoy the festivities."

"Yes, I did notice that *your* last ride over the distance was a bit hazardous to *your* health," she said, unable to keep from making a reference to his battered condition upon arrival at the barn. At the present, there was little indication of his beating except for the lingering line of scab on his lower lip.

"I like a woman with a sense of humor."

"And, I like a man with one, too," she said. "If I were you, though, I'm not too sure I would be so easy to forgive and forget, if...."

She had been on the point of saying, "...you were, indeed, as innocent as you proclaimed." She didn't say that, however, because she didn't want to get into a discussion, especially with him, especially now, as to whether she actually still thought him guilty of killing her bulls. She still felt an inviolate owner-employee responsibility to her ranch hands whom had acted— although spontaneously—to protect her interests.

She was afraid Adriano would immediately pick up on her dangling sentence, so she pointed off into the distance toward a group of trees with trunks gone bright orange to a height of nine or ten feet.

"Cork trees," Adriano informed, apparently willing to let the question of his guilt or innocence not, once again, become a subject of discussion. "The estate has several cork forests. The orange coloring merely means the bark was stripped only a few days ago. After awhile, the orange will go russet, then brown, and finally back to its original gray."

Alyssa only vaguely remembered that legal documents had listed cork as one of the products of her ranch. She had been extremely lax in researching just how a person ran a ranchero of this magnitude. She had procrastinated mainly because she hadn't been all that certain she was going to retain ownership. The stripped bark, though, seemed to indicate that things had not ground to a complete stop while the captain was elsewhere than firmly positioned at the helm. She couldn't help feeling a little guilty that she had arrived on the scene quite as ignorant as she was. But, then, it was only now beginning to dawn on her just how much Lalo Montego had turned over to her keeping.

"I really know nothing of bulls, even less about harvesting cork," she admitted, more to herself than to him.

"Luckily, the people in your employ do know about bulls and cork," he said. "You need merely search them out and express a genuine interest to learn, and they'll be more than happy to teach you all they can."

"Even though I'm a woman?"

"Yes, even though you're a woman. They won't be as biased against you as you might initially imagine. For one, you're an American woman, not Spanish. Few Spaniards, at least those who have worked for my father, can any longer be considered backward enough to imagine an American *señorita* to be the same cloistered female as many of her Spanish counterparts. For two, my father put his stamp of approval on you when he left you the ranch." If any bitterness existed, it didn't come through in his voice. He had merely made an apparent simple statement of fact. "And the people on this ranch owe Lalo Montego a lot. So much, as a matter of fact, that they're not about to question his choice of a successor. Any indication of a permanent owner in residence is going to be welcome. Nothing operates as efficiently as it should without its head— even a ranch like this one."

"Well, that's encouraging," she admitted, wondering if he were only trying to make her feel a bit more confident in a role in which she hadn't yet become confident.

"Besides, as you will soon see, many Spanish women are no longer the sheltered, meek, and mild ladies they have for so long been painted to be by the outside world. Money has, indeed, seemed to have liberated a good many of them. Ladonna Hidalgo, for instance, is a truly liberated woman. The rumor has long existed that she has just as much say in the operation of Hidalgo Hacienda as does her father."

"She's one neighbor, then, who I shall be looking forward to meeting."

"I suppose Joaquín has told you that you've only two ranches close by. There's his ranch, and then there's the ranch of Victoro Isidro. Victoro, by the way probably won't be at the fiesta. The last I heard, he was off buying a new seed bull. But, you'll no doubt have plenty of time to meet him, later; although, at sixty-four he's not apt to be the life of any party. In fact, Joaquín's fiesta will give you an excellent opportunity to become acquainted with most of the aristocracy from Trujillo, Albuquerque, Mérida, and all of the surrounding areas. If Fanuco de Galena isn't enough to bring everyone running, Joaquín is well known for his exceptional hospitality."

The cork trees had given way to barren landscape. The soil was rocky and red. Occasionally, a stream bed appeared, completely devoid of water.

Finally, there was a spot, seemingly in the middle of nowhere, that Adriano pointed out as the end of the property left Alyssa by his father.

"You are now officially on Hidalgo land," he informed. "It won't be long before we reach the hacienda."

It was only five minutes later that an olive forest appeared on the horizon and the car sped toward it. Among the olives was an occasional oak, gnarled trunk and limbs lording it over the smaller, more distorted trees.

The road bisected the forest, and another roadway angled off toward the still hidden ranch house.

Before long, the fiesta element became more than evident as the car sped by a growing number of brightly costumed locals headed in the same direction.

"Joaquín will have turned over most of the immediate hacienda grounds to the villagers," Adriano observed. "God knows, they can use every opportunity for a little fun and games."

Alyssa didn't have to ask why. Her drive from Madrid had taken her though more than one little village. It was easy for her to recall miserable huts without doors except for strings of beads hung to keep out the flies. Not everyone in Spain lived in a hacienda comparable to the one Lalo Montego had bequeathed Alyssa.

The Hidalgo Hacienda was another of those grand old buildings that looked as if it had been erected by some rich grandee—which it had. The building had the appearance of one which would remain standing while every adobe village within miles crumbled into dust. It was a massive structure, all white-washed walls and red brick, surrounded by a high wall that gave access to the main house and the area in which Adriano parked the car.

There were other vehicles already parked, all watched over by several young men who had obviously been paid to make sure nothing happened to the property of the guests. Alyssa had never been all that good at identifying car models, but she knew a Rolls Royce when she saw one (there were three), Mercedes (there were five), and a Cadillac limo (there was one). All the cars were likely expensive, especially, probably, those she couldn't recognize.

Like the Montego Hacienda, the Hidalgo Hacienda was an oasis of trees, flowers, and fountains. It made one quickly forget that for miles all around the desert was in primary control. Within the compound were dazzling colors as plant life ran riot. An abundance of water sprayed from submerged outlets and added a cool misting to the air to keep leaves and lawns free of dust.

"Ah, Adriano!" Joaquín Hidalgo called in greeting. He was standing in the open doorway of the hacienda, greeting the steady line of entering people. "And...." He reached for Alyssa's hand and bowed over it. "... *Señorita* Dunlap. How nice of you to come."

"Looks as if you've brought in every person from miles around," Adriano observed. Several other cars were in the process of parking, all of them filled with passengers.

Beyond the open doorway was another opened double-door that accessed the inner courtyard. Amazingly, there was a cooling breeze blowing through the resulting causeway, bringing with it the smell of fragrant flowers from the central garden.

"Come on, and we'll find Ladonna," Joaquín said. He was speaking mainly to Adriano, although his hand still held Alyssa's fingers. "I think she's with Fanuco who, by the way, is looking forward to seeing you again." He turned his full attention on Alyssa. "And, he's certainly looking forward to meeting my new neighbor."

"Don't you think you should stay positioned at the door to play host?" Adriano suggested.

"I'd miss all of the fun if I did that," Joaquín reminded. "Besides, most everyone is already here. I'll catch the stragglers somewhere during the course of the day or evening. I promise."

He led them through the room and out into the courtyard. Along the way, he stopped briefly to introduce Alyssa to several people Adriano already knew.

"I'll never keep all the names straight," she whispered, after taking her leave, along with Adriano and Joaquín, from yet another group of people.

"Don't worry about it," Joaquín assured. "You'll meet the most important ones on more than one occasion over the next few days, and things will fall into place in no time. In the meantime, Adriano and I will whisper you clues as to identities, so...."

He caught someone's attention across the courtyard and lifted his right arm in signal, his fingers beckoning. "Ah, there they are!" he proclaimed, leading the way toward them.

They hurried passed various people who looked as if they would have enjoyed introductions; Joaquín's attention, though, had narrowed to include no one except the man and the woman heading toward him.

The man was darkly attractive with black hair, square jaw line. He had an exceptional body beneath a well-tailored and obviously expensive suit.

The woman had cascades of black hair; her black eyes were shielded by lush eyelashes that, at closer examination, weren't enhanced by false additions or mascara. What kept her from being a real beauty were lips that were a bit too thin and made her mouth seem somehow too hard, adding a definite brittle edge to an otherwise complete package of attractiveness.

"Adriano!" the man exclaimed, extending a hand to take Adriano's hand, pulling the man to him in a seemingly friendly embrace. "God, it has been a long time, hasn't it?"

"You've become quite famous in the interim, Fanuco," Adriano said, gently pushing Fanuco de Galena at arm's-length and giving him a once-over. "Gotten a little more meat on your bones, too."

"Why don't you two save your remember-whens until all-around introductions are out of the way?" the woman suggested, her eyes taking Alyssa in with a comprehensive glance. Then, not waiting for the men to perform the social amenities, she extended her hand and introduced herself. "I'm Ladonna Hidalgo, and you're Alyssa Dunlap, yes? Alyssa, this is Fanuco de Galena, matador supreme. And, you've met my father. Anyway, he has certainly met you, coming back with reports simply glowing with superlatives."

Alyssa blushed, feeling ill at ease.

"As usual, my father has been right in his assessment. You are, indeed, a very attractive young woman, if I do say so. With those looks and the large tract of land now in your possession, you will undoubtedly soon find yourself surrounded by a coterie of potential suitors. I do hope you'll be able to distinguish the grain from the chaff. If not, check in with me, and I'll be more than happy to give you pointers."

Ladonna was smiling, and her voice sounded as if she were merely bantering; so, why was Alyssa so uncomfortable?

Ladonna released Alyssa's hand and moved closer to Adriano. She raised her right index finger to his face, her blood-red nail pinpointing the small scar still forming on the handsome man's lower lip. "You're looking hardly the worse for wear," she said, her smile widening. "Considering Joaquín's description, I expected you to arrive with all sorts of scarring."

"I heard about that unfortunate incident, Adriano," Fanuco said. "Stupid peasants, yes?" There was certain sarcasm in his voice.

"They were neither peasants nor stupid!" Alyssa announced, reflexively coming to the defense of her ranch hands.

As a result, the three turned their attention in her direction. What could have been turned into an uneasy situation, however, was saved from it by Adriano.

"There were extenuating circumstances," he admitted. "Alyssa is probably right in insinuating her men acted rationally—everything considered."

"You always make such a good martyr, don't you, darling?" Ladonna said, shaking her head and clucking her tongue.

"Don't be a bitch, my dear!" Joaquín chided. Then, he excused himself, saying he had been waiting all morning to get a chance to talk with Homas Falón and finally saw his opportunity.

"And, you two will excuse Adriano and me for a few moments, won't you?" Ladonna said, hooking her arm in Adriano's. "It'll give Alyssa a chance to get better acquainted with our guest of honor."

Adriano smiled his helplessness in the face of Ladonna's persistence; and, promised Alyssa he wouldn't be long.

"They do make a striking couple, don't they?" Fanuco said. He guided Alyssa out of the mainstream of traffic and over to a small bench sitting within a small grape arbor.

"Yes, very," she reluctantly admitted. She noticed how, when Fanuco sat, his left leg touched her right.

"It was indeed unfortunate their engagement was called off, don't you agree?"

"Ladonna Hidalgo and Adriano were engaged?" Her surprise was more than evident. Why shouldn't she be surprised? She *was* surprised! How could Adriano, who had kissed her so passionately, not once have...?

"They *were* engaged," Fanuco emphasized the past tense. "The marriage, of course, became quite impossible when the Montego ranch went to you and not to Adriano. Marriages in this country, at least among the aristocracy, still aren't made for love. They're made for convenience and the merging of land."

"You mean their engagement was broken because Adriano's father didn't leave him the ranch?" She was incredulous. Still a romantic at heart, she found it impossible to reason how any two people could split up because of something as silly as acreage. The idea was medieval!

"The separation was by mutual consent, I assure you," Fanuco promised. "Both realized Ladonna could hardly be expected to marry a man unable to bring with him holdings at least equal to those eventually inherited by his bride."

"That's simply archaic!" Alyssa was still unable to believe it. "Besides, Adriano has assured me his father hardly left him a pauper."

"Oh, his old man left him very well off, to be sure," Fanuco agreed. "In money, that is. Land is what's important in Spain, *Señorita*. Lalo Montego left you the land. The rumor, of course, is that he did so solely to abort the intended marriage of his son."

"I don't understand."

"Well, you're not the only one left curious on that score," Fanuco said with a laugh. He had an attractive face made even more attractive by his lingering smile. "No one really knows what Lalo Montego's objections to the marriage were. For all intents and purposes, he should have found it made in heaven. The Hidalgo land combined with the Montego holdings would have made the biggest spread in Spain. Everybody should have been happy as a lark about the arrangements."

"But, Lalo Montego left the ranch to me?"

"So, you mustn't be too concerned if Ladonna comes across a little cold at times. After all, she does have to see you as the monkey wrench thrown into the works. She's now saddled with Victoro Isidro. And, a man of sixty-four can hardly hold out much invitation—except his land holdings—for someone as obviously young as Ladonna."

Alyssa wasn't sure she understood any of it!

Fanuco motioned for one of the waiters who wandered around the courtyard with a tray of glasses containing champagne and orange juice. He retrieved two and handed one to Alyssa.

"By all means, you mustn't be at all surprised if Joaquín begins making romantic overtures, even if he's old enough to be your father."

"I'm afraid you're completely losing me."

"Am I?" Fanuco asked, dubiously. "Are you sure?"

Alyssa *had* gotten the insinuation that Fanuco de Galena had made in regard to how she should be suspect of any romantic attentions Joaquín Hidalgo might express towards her. She had something Joaquín wanted; something his daughter had been unable to get—the ranch of the deceased Lalo Montego. If Joaquín could charm his way into Alyssa's confidence, despite their obvious age difference, there was a way he could add not only the Isidro property to his coffers, through his daughter's eventual marriage to Victoro Isidro, but, also, snag the Montego estate, via Alyssa. Such success would deliver into his hands the whole giant land-acreage enchilada.

By association, there was more than a slight hint that Alyssa should, also, be on guard against Adriano Montego, for how could a young man who had his marriage plans aborted, because of his father's will, *really* be as unconcerned as he seemed? Wasn't it more likely he was out for some kind of revenge? Wasn't it possible he was out to charm himself into Alyssa's good graces, seduce her, and even marry her—to get the ranch?

Alyssa didn't like the thoughts Fanuco had planted in her head. The next step was for her not to like Fanuco. She was thoroughly prepared to do so, but she found it decidedly difficult to dislike someone so handsome and with such an attractive smile. Still, good looks were only skin-deep.

"Why are you doing this?" she asked. She couldn't figure it out, for the life of her, and if Fanuco didn't know why he was doing it, it was highly unlikely anyone else would.

"Doing what?" His expression was wide-eyed innocence that equally relayed that he knew very well to what she referred.

"I'm not very good at game-playing," she said.

"A pity," he replied, taking a sip of the champagne-orange juice mixture and eyeing her over the rim of his glass, "because, anyone who can't play the game, around here, is liable to end up eaten alive."

"Maybe you would oblige by at least providing me with the rules?"

"Except, there are no rules." His attractive smile still played the corners of his sexy lips. "Not formal ones, that is. Merely the rules of the jungle."

"Surely, you can be more specific than that."

"I suppose I could, but do I really have to be? You can surely see how any attention you receive from either Joaquín or Adriano might be suspect."

"What's confusing to me is why you've said anything. You, Joaquín, and Adriano are all good friends, aren't you?"

"Whatever gave you that idea?" His look was of

genuine astonishment. "Oh, you mean because of our seemingly warm greetings?"

Alyssa was literally at a loss.

"But, I thought...," she began but didn't finish.

"What you have to learn is how to cultivate a knack for seeing beyond facades."

"You're not friends, then?"

"Let's see if I can't clarify it for you a little. I merely think Ladonna, Joaquín, and Adriano, have more than enough already without their gobbling up your inheritance in the bargain. I see no reason why they should have any unfair advantages; although, yes, my motivations, I readily admit, are spawned from pure, unadulterated jealousy."

"Jealousy of Joaquín and Adriano, or both?"

"Even of Ladonna," he added. "Even, for that matter, of you."

"Me?"

"You've all been born with silver spoons in your mouths, haven't you?"

"You weren't?"

"Good God, no! Who has been filling your pretty head with that kind of nonsense?"

"I merely assumed."

"Well, you assumed incorrectly. My father was a ranch hand on the ranchero you now own. I was born in a house with no inside plumbing.

He didn't look as if he were the son of some poor ranch hand.

"What you see—the suit, the expensive boots, the styled hair, the manicured nails—is only one of those façades of which I mentioned. Beneath all of this is the same snot-nosed kid who only got his chance at the bulls because Lalo Montego thought he might be able to spur his own son's interest by offering some competition in the form of a wretched little ragamuffin. So, you see, not even Lalo Montego and I were really friends—in the true sense of the word.

"And did Adriano respond to the competition you offered?"

"The only thing that ever got a response out of Adriano was hatred of his father. That inspired him to give up a promising career in bullfighting rather than possibly becoming one of Spain' greatest matadors. I've always suspected Adriano could have achieved his vengeance on his father far more aptly had he kept on with the bullfighting and eclipsed his father's overrated reputation in the *corrida*."

"His father's reputation was overrated?" Alyssa wasn't all that familiar with bullfighting, but she had always assumed Lalo Montego was first-rate at what he did. To hear Fanuco now insinuate otherwise was surprising.

"He was just slightly more than mediocre in a field

that had sunk to the depths of mediocrity. He looked so good only because his competition was so damned bad."

Alyssa wasn't about to believe a word of that until she checked into the subject a bit more thoroughly. She wasn't at all sure but that what she was hearing, here, was nothing but an undeserved put-down and sour grapes by a very egotistical young man.

"Why did Adriano hate his father so much anyway?" She might as well get Fanuco's ideas on that while he seemed so anxious to spill everything.

"Lalo Montego was not a very nice man with women, Adriano's mother included. Oh, he could be quite charming when he wanted, but he was mean as a rogue bull the majority of the time. Of course, it was his profession which drew women to him like flies to rotten meat. There's something about the *corrida de toros* that makes female blood run hot, yes?"

"I'll have to take your word for it," Alyssa said noncommittally.

"Yes, do."

"What about Lalo's relationship with Joaquín Hidalgo?"

"What about it?"

"I understand they were very good friends."

"Just because Lalo hated women, don't assume for a moment he was homosexual."

"I...ah...wasn't." That notion had never crossed her mind.

Fanuco laughed at her embarrassment, and said, "Oh, it probably would have been far better if he had been. Anyway, it might have given him some sort of inner peace if he had found someone—man or woman—he could enjoy, in and out of the bedroom. His problem was that he really didn't enjoy sex at all. But, knowing it was expected that he should, he just kept searching for enjoyment—never finding it. As for his relation-ship with Joaquín, I assure you it was purely asexual. It wouldn't have lasted as long as it had if Lalo hadn't realized there was no one else in the world he could call a friend, except Joaquín."

"The two remained friendly, then, up until Lalo died in the bullring?"

"Committed suicide in the *corrida*, don't you mean?"

"I beg your pardon."

"It looked like suicide to me," Fanuco said, "and I was there to see it."

"Suicide?"

"Granted, he wasn't anywhere near the performer he had been—which, as I've already said, was never all that good, but he certainly shouldn't have gone down the way he did. It looked very much to me as if he stepped into that horn."

"Why would he have killed himself?"

Fanuco shrugged, and then asked, "But, you were asking about the friendship between Lalo and Joaquín, were you not?"

Alyssa could only nod her head. Fanuco's suggestions had left her pretty much speechless.

"Well, the answer is, yes; at least, it's yes as far as I know. Do you have any reason to believe, they weren't friends to the end?"

She was about to mention what her mother told her, but they were interrupted by Joaquín with a Catholic nun in tow.

"Sister Dominica de Reyalda," Joaquín introduced her to Alyssa. Fanuco already knew Sister Dominica. "It's for her orphanage that Fanuco has so graciously donated the proceeds from the *corrida* he'll be fighting in Madrid next Sunday. The affair has been sold out since the first day the tickets went on sale; aficionados coming from all over the world to see Fanuco de Galena take on all six bulls."

"I'll be sorry to miss it," Alyssa said, wondering if she genuinely meant it. Certainly, it did sound like quite an occasion, but she really wasn't all that sure she would relish seeing someone she knew—even vaguely—face six dangerous bulls in the course of one short afternoon.

"But, of course, you won't miss it!" Joaquín contradicted. "It's quite unthinkable that you should even consider passing up the event."

"Didn't you just say it has been sold out for weeks?"

"Maybe so; however, there's always an extra seat to be scrounged up for a friend of the matador, isn't that right, Fanuco?"

"Of course," Fanuco said, his voice insinuating that money always had, and always would have, the clout to pull strings. "In fact, I should be most insulted if *Señorita* Dunlap didn't attend."

CHAPTER FIVE

"Having fun, are you?" Adriano asked Alyssa.. He had suggested they join the crowd drifting toward the corrals. Fanuco and Joaquín had gone off with several other men to round up heifers for testing with the cape. Adriano had declined their invitation to join them.

"So far, it's been pleasant enough," Alyssa said, acutely aware of his guiding hand resting gently on her left elbow.

"Funny, but I got the definite impression you were looking a bit peaked there for awhile."

"No, I'm fine," she said, though she had been suffering from the discomfort of short bouts of slight nausea. "I guess I ate something that didn't quite agree with me. More likely, I just got a little too much sun. Nothing serious, I assure you."

"I thought, maybe, you'd just found Fanuco distasteful," Adriano said. "Joaquín suggested it might be a big mistake for us to surrender you to him so soon after your arrival."

"What a strange thing to say," Alyssa said.

"You mean that Fanuco didn't take the opportunity to fill your head with all sorts of detrimental tales?"

"About what?"

"You mustn't get the impression that Joaquín, Ladonna, and I aren't genuinely fond of Fanuco. We've all spent a good many years together, you know?"

"He said you and he trained for the bulls together."

"Mmm."

They walked a tree-lined pathway and not alone. Everyone seemed headed in the same direction, but Alyssa and Adriano managed certain isolation by appearing prepared to fend off any infringements upon their private conversation.

"Was your father a good matador?" she asked.

"Isn't 'good' subjective?"

"You know what I mean. Was he a good technician? Did he have good style? However it is that one judges such things in a matador."

"Fanuco told you that my father was rather mediocre, did he?"

"Why would he do that?" Why was she defending the attractive matador, especially since he hadn't once said anything about their discussion being confidential?

"Actually, my father *was* rather mediocre," Adriano admitted, surprising her with his candidness. "Certainly, he wasn't as good as Miguelín, Ortega, or Bienveida. Nor did he have the flamboyance of an El Cordobés. But, he arrived on the scene when the *corrida* hadn't seen a really good matador in years. He resurrected interest that was waning. That's why he became so popular and respected."

"What about Fanuco? I mean, is *he* good?"

"Fanuco is more than good. Fanuco is great." He gave an amused smile. "He did tell you that, too, didn't he?"

"What he said was that you might have been better."

"Yes, I do think he thinks that."

"And?"

Adriano shrugged.

"That's modesty, is it?"

He shrugged again.

"But you *were* good?"

"I was told I had potential. I saw no point in risking my life every Sunday afternoon to prove it."

"If you'd had no money, like Fanuco, would you have taken being a matador more seriously?"

"I wasn't poor like Fanuco, though, was I?"

"But, if you had been?"

"Who knows? I hear poverty can be powerful as motivation."

They walked a little farther in silence.

"Did your father commit suicide?" she asked, after several long seconds of getting up the courage to venture asking. She expected him to be vehement in his denial. Instead, he replied with a chuckle.

"Heard that rumor, too, did you? My goodness, you have been a busy little bee throughout the day."

"That doesn't really answer my question."

"Only because the only person who could answer that question is now dead. I can only tell you that if my father did step in front of that horn, no one has yet been able to come up with any logical explanation as to why. He had everything any man could have wanted. Fame, fortune, land, respect. Even that final *corrida* was a raging success for him—up until the moment of its tragic conclusion. Suicide? I think I would have to veto that notion until someone comes up with a truly logical explanation as to why he would have decided to end his life at that precise moment."

"Fanuco really doesn't like you, does he, despite all of your mutual handshaking and how-good-to-see-you again charades?"

She thought he would deny it. She was surprised... and not for the first time that day...when he didn't.

"He wants to be the best...THE VERY BEST," Adriano said, "not because his competition doesn't want to come out and play, but because he has met and bettered them all."

"He really thinks you might still be better than he is?" she asked, wondering if she were getting the message right.

"Certainly, *I* don't believe I'm better," he said. "I never have. If he has that delusion, he really should get over it."

"So, why doesn't he?"

"A newspaperman once attended a practice session, back in the days when I was still being badgered successfully by my father into taking lessons. The reporter, I'm quite sure, was merely out to make points with my old man, but his resulting newspaper article described me in superlatives that would have you think every great bullfighter in the last century had been resurrected in Lalo Montego's son."

"And, Fanuco *dislikes* Joaquín and Ladonna Hidalgo because he thinks they can outdo him in the *corrida*, too?" Alyssa asked sarcastically.

"Who told you he dislikes Joaquín and Ladonna?"

"He did."

"Well, I suppose that could be a half-truth. There was a time he wanted to marry Ladonna, you know? Joaquín objected, which might certainly give Fanuco reason to hate him. Since there's a thin dividing line between love and hate, maybe Fanuco has even, by now, slipped over the edge as far as Ladonna is concerned, too. God knows, she can be as cold as any fish."

"He loves Ladonna?"

"It's probably 'loved'—past tense—by now. The

lady never did give him much encouragement. How could she? She's been brainwashed since birth into believing that when she marries it must be to increase the Hidalgo land holdings. She couldn't really have been expected to throw aside years of programming to marry for love, especially when Fanuco wasn't all that well established as a matador at the time he proposed marriage to her."

"She loved him?"

"My god, we *are* full of questions!"

"Humor me awhile longer, please."

"To expect what from you, next?" He eyed her if he'd just caught her with her hand in the cookie jar. "Some questions, maybe, to do with you having heard I was once engaged to Ladonna, too? Fanuco possibly having suggested to you that my split-up with her was because you came along and got the ranch instead of me?"

"Was that the reason?"

"I suppose it was," he admitted. "Our marriage was intended for the sole purpose of joining our two ranches. When that became impossible, there was no longer any reason to proceed."

"Love isn't reason enough among the Spanish aristocracy?"

"My dear, as far as I'm concerned, love is probably the most ideal reason for two people to become engaged and eventually marry. At the time we're discussing, though, neither Ladonna nor I was in love with anyone, including with each other. Nor were we contemplating any such love; so, there seemed little reason why we shouldn't oblige her father's wishes and tie the knot."

"A loveless marriage for the sake of convenience?" Alyssa continued to be shocked by the very idea.

"It became even more attractive when I realized how my father, despite all of his mouthing to the contrary, really didn't want the marriage to happen."

"Why didn't he?"

"I haven't the foggiest."

Alyssa hadn't run out of questions, and she was certain Adriano hadn't run out of answers, but they'd reached the *plaza de toros*, built by the Hidalgo family as part of their estate complex, and they'd became a more intimate part of the converging crowd.

The private bullring was not an affectation of the Hidalgo family. It was a standard fixture on any ranch used for raising bulls for the *corrida*, including the one Alyssa now owned. Mainly, they were used to test heifers for their bravery, since it was thought by breeders that bravery, or lack thereof, was passed from cows to their calves.

Adriano led Alyssa to her seat.

In the circular arena below them, Joaquín, Fanuco, and several other men were herding heifers into stalls.

Each animal, amid a commotion of opening and closing gates, seemed nervously anticipating its eventual entrance into the *corrida*.

Alyssa took a momentary lull to get in one more question. "What's Fanuco doing here if he doesn't care for any of you?"

"It's a love-hate relationship," Adriano said, as if he doubted he could ever get her to understand an aspect of the Spanish male character which had to be forever a mystery to an outsider. "After all, he's kind of an adopted member of my family. On a more obvious and more understandable level, he's here because we can help him."

"Help him do what?" She was afraid Adriano was on the verge of stopping right there.

"He's very ambitious. He wants to be accepted not only in the bullring but in society, too. Probably because he's sure that his not having been a member was the only reason Joaquín objected to his marriage with Ladonna."

"Was it?"

"Not *just* the matter of social position. Again, land was the deciding factor. Ladonna could hardly marry someone without social standing *or* land, not when she could marry *both* by having Victoro Isidro."

Alyssa was tempted to ask if Ladonna would have ended up engaged to Victoro Isidro if Lalo Montego had made other provisions in his will. However, she lost her nerve at that moment and decided to satisfy her curiosity, instead, as regarded another point.

"Just what exactly are you getting out of this?" she asked. "I mean, I see the advantages to Fanuco in his chumming around with the aristocracy, but what's to be gained from your side?"

"Joaquín and Ladonna are patrons of Sister Dominica's orphanage, and its invaluable publicity to be seen as having been successful in getting Spain's principal up-and-coming *matador de toros* to volunteer for the event."

"What about you? Are you a patron of the orphanage, too?"

"I'm just returning favors owed Joaquín for his having offered me his hospitality when my father kicked me out on my ass. Fanuco is really only here to show off in front of me, you know. It's his need to do that, by way of proving to me just how much better a matador he's become than I could have ever hoped to be that allows him to have been maneuvered into attending not only today's little fiesta but his real money-making performance in the plaza in Madrid next week."

"Do you think it fair to have tapped Fanuco's insecurities?"

"Alyssa, it is for a good cause. It's not as if any of us are out to shovel the proceeds into our own coffers.

Hell, this is being done purely for charity so that Sister Dominica won't have to send any of her charges out onto the street. Besides, the publicity hasn't hurt Fanuco's career any. It's more likely done it a world of good."

The gentleman sitting on the other side of Adriano took the opportunity to make himself known. After which, Adriano made formal introductions, and Alyssa found herself caught up in a three-way conversation that included everything from the champagne used in the breakfast punch to the lineage of the heifers herded into the pens.

In the meantime, most of the men who had been moving the cows had vacated the ring in favor of seats in the stands. A few—like Joaquín and Fanuco—had taken up positions immediately behind the barriers.

Ladonna Hidalgo sat not too far from Alyssa, amid a circle of obvious male admirers. By turning slightly to her right, Alyssa could unobtrusively catch flashes of Ladonna's white teeth and sexy tosses of the woman's cascading black hair.

However, Alyssa's attention was soon centered entirely on the ring when a heifer erupted into the circular enclosure. The animal raised a storm of dust as it proceeded to charge into the emptiness. At just a hint of Joaquín's body from behind the edge of the barrier, the animal charged.

The crowd roared approval of the animal's bravura, and it did so, yet again, as two men appeared without capes just long enough to send the heifer chasing after them. One of the men barely managed to regain concealment ahead of the animal's charge.

Finally, Fanuco stepped out, brandishing a magenta-and-yellow cape that immediately caught the heifer's attention, and the animal rushed it.

Alyssa was fascinated by just how fast the animal moved, charging the cape as if it had forever been its life-long enemy. In fact, she could hardly believe the heifer had so quickly covered the space separating it from the young matador.

The cape swirled again, and the animal moved with it around the statue-like posturing of Fanuco. The crowd shouted its approval.

"Fantastic!" Alyssa mumbled, hardly realizing she had put her thoughts into words.

"And, that's only a heifer he's working," Adriano said, seeming amused by Alyssa's impressionability. "Fanuco stands just as solidly when he has a full-grown bull of over a thousand pounds, complete with sharp horns, dancing around him."

The next few minutes, Alyssa watched while Adriano kept up a running commentary, pointing out the good points of Fanuco and the heifer.

"The cow can determine its offspring," Adriano said.

"This heifer obviously comes from a good strain. See the way she doesn't give up, just keeps on charging the cape, even though Fanuco snaps the cloth away from her each and every time?"

Fanuco finished with the heifer, ushering it out with a flurry of cape work. Then, he began practicing with yet another animal allowed entrance at a nod from Joaquín Hidalgo. This second animal was as spirited as the first. Fanuco cape-passed this one as expertly as he had the one before it.

"Ole!" a man three places away from Alyssa screamed in appreciation and was echoed immediately by others.

"Imagine how hundreds of people sound in Madrid's *Plaza de Toros* when it's a real bull and not merely a heifer performing to Fanuco de Galena's tune," Adriano suggested.

Alyssa tried to imagine it, but she found it hard to do. What Fanuco was doing with that cow was more beautiful than she had ever imagined it could be.

The second heifer exited the ring amid sounds of genuine appreciation for what Fanuco had accomplished with it.

Alyssa was actually looking forward to seeing yet a third animal released to match its skills with the matador.

Fanuco, though, had moved to a position almost

directly below her and called up something.

At first, Alyssa thought he was calling to her. Didn't matadors sometimes dedicate their bulls to friends and acquaintances in the stands? But, this wasn't a regular bullfight. There weren't even any bulls. And Fanuco wasn't talking to her but was calling up to Adriano. As soon as Alyssa realized that, she turned to Adriano and saw his expression that included discernable taut movements of the muscles along his jaw line.

"What did he say?" she asked. At the same time, she already knew what Fanuco had said. Adriano and everyone else in the bullring knew, too. Since her question was superfluous, she really didn't expect Adriano to answer—and he didn't.

"Well?" Fanuco shouted. The only other sounds in the place were the heifers moving in their pens. "Surely, that's not too much to ask for a good cause, is it?"

Alyssa did some fast mental computations. She still hadn't adjusted to thinking entirely in Spanish, but, if her figures were correct, Fanuco had just offered to contribute the equivalent $4,000 U.S. cash to Sister Dominica's orphanage fund if Adriano would cape-pass just one heifer a few times before the assembled crowd.

The arena went even quieter. Even the animals seemed to sense something in the works, stopping their pawing of the ground and fastening large brown eyes upon Adriano in the stands. Alyssa was sure a pin could have been heard dropping if someone would have just bothered to drop one.

She didn't know what Adriano would do. She did know that whatever it was, she was furious with Fanuco for having put the man who she was with in this untenable situation.

"That's an awfully lot of money to pay for an amateur performance," Adriano finally called back.

"Yes, it is," Fanuco agreed. "However, it's all for a good cause, is it not?"

"You won't expect too much?" Adriano asked.

Alyssa wondered if he was actually going to be sucked in by Fanuco's baiting. On the other hand, what else could he do? It seemed like a simple enough request. After all, these weren't bulls. Nor, was Adriano a rank amateur; he did have the background necessary to put on a fairly decent show. And since it was money for charity, it would have seemed a little spoiled-sport of him to refuse.

"We all realize you're a bit rusty," Fanuco conceded. "We don't expect perfection."

"Then, what can I do but accept your kind donation?" Adriano said.

In reply, the stadium erupted with screams and shouts of encouragement. Even Alyssa found herself clapping delightedly. It wasn't as if she was cheering a

Christian being sent to the lions. Certainly, there was little danger for Adriano down there in this ring.

"If you'll excuse me, then, it seems I have suddenly become part of the entertainment," Adriano said, scooting past her en route to the steps leading down to the barriers.

Alyssa used her right hand to push hair off her forehead, realizing that she was exceptionally excited. Her heart pounded. Her flesh flushed and, then, went damp with perspiration. She could sense, too, that all those around her were excited, as well. Even Ladonna Hidalgo sat physically forward in her seat, her eyes avidly following Adriano's progression.

Most of these people had never seen Adriano Montego in any bullring. They had heard that some experts had once predicted he would go far in the profession, but they, also, knew he had rebelled against such predictions and against his father's wishes. It was, indeed, a treat to get a peek at the greatness which might have been. If these weren't real bulls, that made little difference. It was a treat, nonetheless. So much so that many from the audience would have gladly chipped into the charitable pot if Fanuco had only suggested it.

Adriano reached the dirt enclosure, having climbed over the low wall separating it from the stands. He said a few low words to Fanuco before Joaquín arrived to separate the two of them, taking Adriano off to one side for more hurried conversation.

Obviously, Joaquín was more than a little upset and wanted Adriano to know that he certainly had nothing whatsoever to do with any of these theatrics. He was well aware of how embarrassing for Adriano it would have been to refuse Fanuco's invitation. As host, Joaquín was furious at what had rightfully looked, and been, a serious breach of etiquette and his hospitality.

Adriano, though, seemed prepared to live up to his commitment. He walked back to Fanuco and took the magenta and yellow cape from him. As he took possession, he fanned it in a series of intricate flourishes that had colored material billowing all around him; there was thunderous applause.

Alyssa surprised herself by jumping to her feet and joining in. Possibly, she was demonstrative as a means of chastising Fanuco for having maneuvered Adriano into such a corner. Fanuco must have recognized how the crowd was coming across far more excited by the prospect of seeing a bit of cape work by Adriano that by seeing Fanuco de Galena pass a third heifer—despite Fanuco having the better reputation, what with his participation in some major bullfights. That Adriano hadn't appeared in the bullring for years couldn't be told from the clamorous response he continued to receive.

Alyssa only hoped Adriano wasn't so rusty he

wouldn't be able to put up a halfway decent show. If he could just come through respectably, that would really show Fanuco had made a wrong move in forcing any comparisons.

Adriano signaled for silence and was given it only after an extended session of more handclapping and cheers. When quiet finally did come, Adriano nodded to Joaquín.

"Open the gate!" Joaquín ordered, and the gate swung open, admitting another heifer into the ring.

It looked larger than those which had come before it. Also, it moved with genuinely astonishing speed, running first here and then there, charging thin air while Adriano watched it.

Meanwhile, Fanuco watched Adriano. Positioned behind the barrier, Fanuco must have wondered if he hadn't miscalculated. Likely, he'd never really expected Adriano to accept the challenge. He couldn't help but notice—by the way Adriano was working the cape—that the man had seemingly forgotten very little, if anything, of their early learning sessions.

Adriano held the cape, twitching it slightly to get the heifer's eye. The animal dashed pell-mell toward the movement, delighted finally to have something substantial on which to vent anger and frustration. It seemed little fazed that the target was soon ripped from in front of it. It merely relocated the movement which Adriano expertly provided and charged again... and again...and again. Five, six, seven times, the heifer doubled back on itself, running at the offending cape that was entirely under Adriano's control.

At times, the man and the animal were merged within the colorful swirl of the cloth. Man and animal became as if one in a stylistic ballet that held Alyssa rooted to her seat. Everyone else was rooted, too. Adriano Montego wasn't disappointing them. It made no difference that it wasn't a thousand-pound bull that he was working, there in the ring. Any aficionado, and there were many in the audience, could take what he or she saw and transpose it to another time and another place to conjure just how it might be if the heifer were a bull with the stamina and horns to kill the man who played it.

Men and women more experienced than Alyssa at detecting the qualities of a man with a cape could tell they were seeing something special. Adriano was, indeed, the son of Lalo Montego.

"Enough!" Joaquín announced finally. Although he would have liked to see more, he figured Fanuco had gotten more than his money's worth.

Adriano obeyed the announced ending of the exhibition. He stepped back. A gate was opened, and a man offered himself as a momentary distraction for the heifer. The animal charged the new target, shooting through the open gate which was closed behind it.

The applause was deafening.

Adriano gave a modest bow and turned the cape over to Joaquín who passed it on to Fanuco with a comment that was lost in the cacophony.

Stopping for handshakes and slaps on his back, Adriano worked his way back up to the seat he had vacated next to Alyssa.

"You were truly fantastic" she said exuberantly, feeling giddy and more than a little light-headed. She expected him to sit down, surprised when he didn't.

"I'm afraid I have to leave now," he said, nodding this way and that as the applause and congratulations continued.

Alyssa was sure she misheard. She couldn't imagine why he would want to remove himself so quickly from such a moment of personal triumph.

"I'm sure Joaquín can arrange transportation back to your place for you, if you'd prefer to stay on," he continued.

"You're actually leaving?" she asked.

"It was a mistake for me to succumb to Fanuco's goading," he said. "If I stay now, it won't end at just this. Fanuco, you know, was expecting me to make an ass of myself."

Alyssa had actually forgotten all about Fanuco. She made it a point to search him out now. The matador was in the arena, looking duly upstaged and obviously resenting it.

"I'll leave with you, of course," she said, "but shouldn't we tell Joaquín we're going?"

"He'll understand without being told," Adriano assured. "So, let's exit as gracefully as possible before Fanuco carries this charade even farther."

The crowd gave a collective groan as it realized Adriano was maneuvering for Alyssa and his exit. When he gave them the parting wave that verified his departure, it was greeted by yet another collective groan even louder than the one which preceded it.

Joaquín quickly diverted most everyone's attention by motioning for the release of yet another heifer into the bullring.

Heads turned, and Adriano took hold of Alyssa's hand and led her out of the arena and back onto the tree-lined pathway that finally had them at the car.

"You really didn't have to leave with me, you know?" he said pausing before opening the car door for her. "Joaquín would have been more than happy to have seen you home."

"That's okay. I think I've had more than enough excitement for one day, anyway." Her body was still filled with spreading warmth that warned she may have had way too much exposure, during the course of the day, to the hot Spanish sun.

Once they were on the road, speeding through bleak countryside beyond the small oasis of greenery that contained the Hidalgo Hacienda, Alyssa waited for Adriano to break the silence.

"I really shouldn't have done that to Fanuco, you know?" he said finally.

"Done what?" She found it ironic that he might actually imagine Fanuco de Galena hadn't gotten just what he deserved.

"Taken away even a bit of his glory."

"The way I see it, there was very little you could have done to avoid it. Anyone there can verify he left you very little choice."

Without saying anything, Adriano gave the impression he wasn't sure he could agree.

"Well, do you see any way you could have gotten out of doing what you did?" she pressed.

He didn't immediately answer. By the time he got around to saying something at all, he'd given every impression the subject was closed.

"I knew he would pull that stunt," he said.

"You knew?" No doubt, that revelation was surprising.

"I told you before: Fanuco and I grew up together. I can read him like a book."

"You knew?" she repeated.

"Not only did I know, but I practiced for the occasion. I sneaked out at nights all the while I was staying with Joaquín. I practiced and got in shape just so I could go out there, today, and make him look foolish."

"Well, then," Alyssa said after a long pause of her own, "I'd say you did nothing more than beat Fanuco at his own game. He was out to make you look ridiculous; turnabout is fair play."

"What he was out to do was show the world that the rumors about me weren't true, and that I wasn't nearly as good as I had once been billed. That he, by comparison was better and always had been. I deprived him of that moment, letting my ego convince me it was more important for me to look good than it was for him to look better than I did. When it shouldn't have been important to me at all, don't you see? Bullfighting isn't my life like it is Fanuco's."

"What *is* your life?"

He shrugged.

"You did look mighty good out there, Adriano," she said. "I don't even know that much about bullfighting, and I could tell."

"I should have gone out there and simply put up on decent show, you know? No one really expected any kind of razzle-dazzle. They knew I was out of practice. They would have appreciated my just putting out the effort—for charity and all. But, oh, no, I had to come off looking like someone who stepped into a bullring cold and outmaneuvered a matador who had never dreamed he had to be anything but passable at a local fiesta. I've made people wonder...I've made Fanuco wonder...how good I can be with a little practice. When unbeknownst to them, I'd already practiced on the sly."

"Fanuco still shouldn't have insisted." Alyssa was quite convinced that Fanuco was entirely to blame, and she refused to be dissuaded.

Adriano pulled the car over to the side of the road and stopped it. He turned in the seat toward her, reached for her, and kissed her.

Alyssa knew it was going to happen before he did it, and she did nothing whatsoever to stop it. She wanted it to happen. She wanted to experience the feel of his lips, and the gentle probing of his tongue.

He broke the kiss finally and ran his tongue back and forth over his lips that held a smile "That was actually quite marvelous," he said and held her even closer.

"I agree with you, there," she admitted. At the same time, she wondered if the way she felt was based more upon the excitement she'd experienced during his time in the bullring than on anything else.

Oh, she had allowed him to kiss her before, and she had kissed him in return, but this time was different. It was almost as if her whole body was somehow set on fire and burning up all of her energy.

He kissed her again, and his mouth lingered. The

pressure of his lips forced hers gently apart. He ran the fingers of his right hand upward through her hair. His mouth left hers, found her neck and kissed that.

Alyssa felt the resulting rush of heat all of the way to her toes. She put her right hand on the nape of his neck and allowed her fingers to progress into his black hair.

"I think I love you," he whispered against her throat, his lips warm and sensuous as they moved against her flesh.

And Alyssa wanted him to love her. It suddenly made no difference whatsoever—at least at that moment— that Fanuco de Galena had warned her that Adriano might not want anything from her except the hacienda his father had left her.

CHAPTER SIX

Quite suddenly, Alyssa realized her sheets were wet with her perspiration. She threw back whatever was covering her and came to a sitting position, feeling a little dizzy with the movement. She felt her forehead with her hand, wondering if she had a temperature. She was hot, all right, but that could have had several explanations.

She glanced at the clock on the bedside table and realized it had been less than an hour since Adriano had kissed her a final good night and gone to his own room. She wondered what it would be like to go to bed each night and have him beneath the covers with her, his warm, hard flesh pressed against her.

In a sudden shift of thought, she wondered if he had kissed her, loved her, said he loved her, not because of any real need inside of him for her as a person, but only because she had something he wanted—the ranch his father, for some inexplicable reason, had left to her instead of to him. Was the only reason he was involved with her because he could no longer have Ladonna

Hidalgo? He had insisted there had never been any love relationship between Ladonna and him, and that he had cultivated that engagement and those wedding plans only because he had intuitively sensed his father was against them. Yet, did any of that hold water? Why would Lalo Montego have disapproved of something so obviously beneficial to all sides? Certainly, he couldn't have looked upon the merging of his bloodline with that of an old friend as something distasteful. Certainly, he shouldn't have objected to the joining by marriage of two of the largest estates in the region.

If Lalo and Joaquín had been feuding, why was Alyssa's mother the only one who seemed to know anything about it? Surely, Fanuco would have had no reason to have kept that from Alyssa.

She was tremendously thirsty. She reached for the pitcher and glass beside her bed and was startled to find that she had already all but emptied the former during the course of less than an hour. She drank what water was left but found it not nearly enough.

She got out of bed, put on her slippers and her robe, and went downstairs.

In the kitchen, she found some milk, feeling very much like a child clandestinely raiding the refrigerator. She had never done such things, even when young, and, even now, felt guilty in doing so.

She took the milk into the den which was a fairly

large room filled with overstuffed chairs and lots of books on lots of shelves. She sat down in one of the wing-back chairs and let her mind begin running back over much the same things which had kept her sleepless within her room at the top of the stairs.

Did Adriano love her? Did she love him? Was all of this just a dream? Why had Lalo Montego left the ranch to her? Why had...?

The phone rang beside her. Automatically, she reached for it and lifted its receiver from its hook.

"Yes," she spoke into the mouthpiece, only then wondering who could possibly be calling at that time of the night on the landline.

"Alyssa?"

"Joaquín?" She thought she recognized the voice on the other end of the line.

"Is Adriano there, my dear? I keep getting his answering service on his cell phone."

"He's upstairs asleep. I'm downstairs only because I got thirsty."

"Maybe you had better wake him, Alyssa," Joaquín said. "I'm afraid this is rather important. It's Fanuco, my dear. I'm afraid, after the two of you left here, this afternoon, he did something very foolish and got badly hurt in result."

While she could imagine some damage done by the heifers, she couldn't imagine anything so bad that....

"He insisted we bring in one of the bulls, Alyssa. He bought and paid for it, and, then, had it turned loose in the ring. I'm afraid it all ended up very badly."

"My God!" She felt ill to her stomach. She had known Adriano had been afraid Fanuco would do something crazy, but she had never dreamed it would have gone this far.

"Fanuco is asking for Adriano. Despite everything, the two are almost family."

"I'll wake him, at once, of course."

"Just tell him to come here. The doctor says Fanuco can't be moved."

"Yes, of course."

"Alyssa?"

"Yes?"

"Are you feeling all right, my dear?"

"Me? Yes. Why?"

"You just sound kind of funny. It's probably the connection."

"Yes, I'm sure it's that."

She replaced the telephone. Having completely forgotten her milk, she left the glass on the table, her legs feeling as if they were made of lead.

She took the stairs slowly and headed down the hallway at the top. She stopped by Adriano's door, leaning against it.

My God, she was tired!

She heard nothing whatsoever from behind the door. So, she knocked. Getting no response, she knocked again. Silence.

She wrapped the fingers of her right hand around the knob and twisted. The door came open a crack.

"Adriano?" She pushed the door a bit more and stuck her head inside. "Adriano?"

She could see his empty bed bathed in moonlight which entered the room through the window. She pushed the door completely open.

The bed hadn't been slept in. Its bedspread had been turned down, but the sheets beneath weren't even wrinkled. She thought Adriano might be in the adjoining bathroom, but its door was wide open, and its lights out.

She stepped back into the hallway and stood stock still and listened. There was nothing to hear except the sounds of the night—and her decidedly erratic breathing.

So, where was he?

She went back down to the den and called Joaquín.

"I really don't know where Adriano is, Joaquín," she confessed. "He's not in his room."

"He seems to have taken to strolling about at night," Joaquín said. "I noticed it while he was staying here."

Alyssa didn't mention how Adriano's nightly walks at the Hidalgo Hacienda were probably to practice bullfighting techniques on the sly. It was highly doubtful that was what Adriano was up to now.

"Just have him get over here as soon as he can, when he does get back, won't you, Alyssa? I don't like to be an alarmist, but the doctor does say there could be serious complications."

When she hung up, she waited, listening for any sounds that might tell her that Adriano had returned.

She waited until she got cold. Then, she told herself she would be far wiser to go upstairs and wait in the comfort of her own bed. She got up, but her legs simply refused to support her. She sat down again.

What was happening to her?

Mara woke her in the morning, frankly appalled to find her mistress apparently had slept in a downstairs chair most of the night. Mara's additional venting of displeasure, amid much tongue clucking and fore-telling of pneumonia likely on its way, was interrupted by a knock on the front door.

"She's asleep," Alyssa heard Mara say to whomever was at the door.

"I'm afraid you'll have to wake her, then," a man's voice said. "This is important."

"Ramón?" Alyssa asked, having made it far enough out of her chair to get a good view of her foreman in the doorway.

"I'm sorry to disturb you, *Señorita*," Ramón said

apologetically, "but last night, there were three more bulls shot. And this was left pinned on one of the carcasses."

He held out his right hand, and Alyssa took the envelope. She opened it, wondering why her fingers didn't seem able to operate in quite the way her brain commanded them.

"'Go back where you belong,'" she read aloud from the note which was written in a childish scrawl, "'or, it won't be only your bulls which end up dead.'"

Mara gave an audible gasp.

"Who could possibly be doing this?" Alyssa asked, admittedly upset. Actually, she felt physically ill to her stomach.

"Do what?" Adriano asked.

He'd come up on the porch and was standing in the doorway which had been left open when Ramón stepped into the house.

"You!" Alyssa accused. "You did this, didn't you?"

"Did what?" Adriano asked.

"Out killing my bulls, again, were you?" she said, hearing her voice get hysterical in the process. "Afraid to kill them face to face in the bullring, are you? Afraid you'll get gored like poor Fanuco, but not above going out and blowing them away with a rifle, are you?"

"What's this all about?" Adriano asked.

Ramón eyed Adriano suspiciously. Mara looked

merely concerned for Alyssa.

"Just get out of here!" Alyssa commanded. "Go back to the Hidalgo Hacienda and see what's happened to that poor man you showed up in the bullring to salve your masculine ego."

"Fanuco?"

"He really wanted to show you up," she continued. Her voice was reaching an ever higher crescendo with each passing word. She wondered what she was saying. It didn't really seem to be her talking at all. "After we left yesterday, he fought a real bull that laid open his guts. When Joaquín called to tell you, you were out killing three more of my bulls with a gun."

"Fanuco gored?" Adriano asked, as if he really hadn't yet made heads or tails of anything Alyssa was saying.

"He's probably already dead!" she screamed.

Adriano did a quick about-face and headed for one of the cars parked outside.

"You coward!" Alyssa shouted after him. "You coward...coward...coward!"

Then, she collapsed into a heap on the floor, and would have probably badly banged her head if Ramón hadn't moved so quickly to cushion her fall.

CHAPTER SEVEN

Alyssa had lost all sense of time and place. She thought for sure she had to be dreaming; there was simply no way she could logically fit her mother into any valid reality. Yet, there was something startlingly real about the woman standing at the curtains and looking out over the courtyard beyond the balcony.

"Mother?"

Karen Dunlap Montego Lewis Svaltzson gave a start and turned toward her daughter on the bed. Despite what the doctors had said about Alyssa merely being the latest victim of a "bug" many *turistas* caught while in Spain, Karen had been positive her daughter was never going to regain consciousness. And Karen was decidedly worried about this horrible mix-up involving Ty which only a conscious Alyssa could clear up. Karen had visited the jail twice in Trujillo, and these barbarians had beaten the poor man senseless.

"Alyssa?" Karen asked, wondering if she wasn't simply imagining, via wishful thinking, that her daughter's eyes were finally open and Alyssa was attempting to sit up. She left the window and hurried over. "Oh, my darling, is it really you, back among the living?"

"What happened?" Alyssa was acutely aware that everything looked and smelled very much like a sick room. So, who had been ill?

"You had me scared to death," Karen said. "Thank goodness you've finally come around."

"Have I been ill?"

"Darling, you haven't said anything coherent for the last four days. I've been frantic."

"How nice of you to come, mother," Alyssa said, looking around for something to eat; she was famished, "but as fit as I feel, now, I'm sure it couldn't have been anything too serious."

"It was a virus," Karen informed. "I was assured a lot of people get it, and get over it, with bed rest, but that was of little consolation, let me tell you." She fluffed the pillows behind Alyssa's back and head.

"How did they contact you?" Alyssa saw an orange on a saucer by the telephone and reached for it and the knife beside it. More often than not, even Alyssa had trouble tracking down her mother.

"Ty called me, darling."

"Ty Gordman?"

"He was in quite a state."

"I'm afraid I don't understand." Alyssa used the knife blade to score the orange rind for easier peeling.

"How did he find out I was sick?" She stopped what she was doing. She remembered what happened just prior to her collapse. Had she actually said all of those horrible things to Adriano? She must have been made hysterical by whatever the "bug" she'd caught. Surely, Adriano must have realized that.

And, what about Fanuco?

In the interim, Karen wasn't talking about Adriano or Fanuco but about Alyssa's ex-fiancé.

"Ty did what?" Alyssa was jerked back to the then and there.

"You simply can't imagine how they've been treating him. They beat him. With clubs. The last time I was there, he could hardly see out of one eye. I told them to let him out, but they won't do anything without your say, and you've been completely incoherent."

"Back up a little, mother." Momentarily, Alyssa forgot the orange in her lap as well as her hunger for it which had prompted her to begin peeling it.

"Now, Alyssa, I know how horrible it must sound, but you can't blame the man, can you? I mean, he loves you, darling. He does."

"You're telling me Ty shot and killed all of those bulls?"

"He merely wanted you back home with him where you belong." Karen reached forward to smooth a stray lock of hair out of Alyssa's eyes. "Granted, he might have resorted to fairly unorthodox methods, but...."

"Ty...killed...*my*...bulls?"

"You would have thought he'd killed a whole village of people, the way the authorities are acting," Karen said. "I tell you, Alyssa, we simply must get that poor man out of that horrible jailhouse as soon as humanly possible."

"And the threatening note I received?" Alyssa wondered if this wasn't all fantasy after all—nothing but a macabre nightmare. "Did Ty write that, too?"

"I'm afraid that little note does seem to have the police rather upset," Karen admitted. "Even when I tried to explain to them how it was all part of a harmless lover's scheme, they refused to budge. You would think hot-blooded Spaniards would appreciate the pathos of this little tale of passion. Or, is it only the Italians who are hot-blooded?"

"Mother, Ty, in that note, actually threatened my life!"

"Come now, Alyssa," Karen cajoled. "You and I both know he wouldn't hurt a hair on your head. The only reason he did any of this is because he was sure you found him unromantic and a bit wish-washy."

"Now, I just find him crazy!"

"Crazy with love," Karen dismissed, as if Alyssa was somehow missing the point. "I'm sure he would have had second thoughts had he known the authorities were incapable of understanding such affairs of the heart. Do you know that they kept him for over two days before he could even make a phone call?"

"How did they find out he was killing my bulls?"

Karen glanced nervously around the room, as if she suspected it contained concealed listening devises.

"Apparently, your foreman staked out a bull and brought Ty to it like some poor tiger falls for the ploy offered up by a decoy goat. You were unconscious, and poor Ty was beaten senseless and hauled off to that dreadful jail in Trujillo where he's still beaten regularly as clockwork."

Alyssa remembered how badly Adriano looked after her men had finished with him, and she could just imagine how Ty looked, about now, after having been caught red-handed.

Poor, innocent Adriano! Alyssa had made horrible accusations the morning of her collapse, all false. "What about Adriano Montego?" She tried to appear casual. She began a renewed effort at peeling the orange.

"He called a couple of times to see how you were," Karen said. "Right now, though, he's in Madrid."

"Madrid?"

"Some kind of charity event, as I understand it. He's actually going to fight six bulls in one afternoon, someone said."

"Adriano is going to fight them? Adriano Montego?"

"Surely, you don't find that so surprising, do you, my dear? He is Lalo Montego's son, after all."

"But Fanuco de Galena was scheduled to do it."

"Oh, you mean that poor young man laid up at the Hidalgo Hacienda?"

"He's not dead, then?"

"He's well on his way to a complete recovery, but he's certainly not up to fighting even one bull for awhile yet. Since all of the tickets to the performance were sold out weeks in advance, Adriano graciously volunteered to step in."

"What day is it today?"

"It's Thursday, darling. There's plenty of time for you to get well enough to attend the performance if you so desire. As a matter of fact, Ladonna and Joaquín Hidalgo stopped by just this morning to see how you were doing and to say they and Victoro Isidro are flying to Madrid for the occasion. They're saving seats for us, although I can't imagine why you'd want to go see such a thing. Even when I was married to Lalo, I found the whole spectacle more than a little distasteful."

"At least the bulls have a better chance in the arena than with a man holding a rifle to their heads," Alyssa reminded. She broke the orange in half and relayed one of its juicy segments to her mouth.

"Yes, of course, there is that," Karen reluctantly

admitted. She walked back to the curtains which were now gently blowing in a slight breeze incoming from the courtyard.

"My goodness, being back here brings back old memories," she said, obviously proposing to move their conversation elsewhere. "I don't remember things quite so green. Certainly, I don't remember it so quiet. Then, it never was quiet when I was here. Lalo always had scads of people milling around." She pulled back the edge of the fluttering cloth, allowing a ray of sunshine to enter through the breach and bathe a section of her face.

Alyssa watched her. She could well see how Lalo Montego might have, at one time, been attracted to the woman. Alyssa's mother was still very attractive. Granted, there were wrinkles at the corners of her eyes not completely muted by her last facelift, and her still luxurious hair wasn't naturally that shade of attractive blonde, but she was still striking, nevertheless.

"Lalo Montego was really a very wretched man," Karen said, turning back to her daughter. "In retrospect, I don't know what I ever saw in him. Certainly, he didn't like women. Certainly, he didn't like men. He had to have been the most destructive human being I ever met. Maybe that was part of his attraction, like a flame that draws moths in to their destruction."

She let out a long sigh. Obviously, she wasn't at all

sure she liked being back—even now that Lalo was long dead and buried.

"Tell me about Adriano Montego," Karen said, coming back to the bed and sitting down on the edge of it. To occupy her hands, she began picking up the segments of orange peel Alyssa had discarded on the bedspread. She piled them neatly on the saucer. "Joaquín says Adriano is nothing like his father."

"Joaquín said that?"

"'You'd never know he was Lalo's son at all,' is how he put it. I rather had the impression he hoped I would pass on that bit of information to you. Fond of Adriano, are you?"

"Adriano and his father are about as different as Ladonna Hidalgo and her father," Alyssa said in order to get the conversation off her feelings for Adriano; she wasn't sure of them herself without having to try and explain them to her mother. As soon as she said what she said, though, she felt a slight twinge of guilt. She'd had very little to do with Ladonna since meeting her. Certainly, she didn't know enough about the woman to be making bitchy observations about Ladonna and her father.

"Well, yes, I can very well see where anyone might see the difference between Ladonna and Joaquín," Karen admitted. "At least that, though is easily explained away, isn't it?"

Alyssa found her mother's reply decidedly curious. "Easily explained away?"

"Oh, yes, certainly," Karen said. A small smile (although, obviously, not one of amusement) played on her lips. She turned more toward her daughter and smiled more genuinely. "But, what possible good can come of my stirring up that smelly barrel of fish all of these years later?"

"I don't understand, mother," Alyssa's curiosity was genuinely whetted.

"Nor is there any reason why you should understand, my dear," Karen said, patting the bedspread ballooned over her daughter's legs. "Your mother has no right to foist all of her unhappy memories on you."

"Sometimes it helps to talk about them," Alyssa prodded.

"Hmm," Karen hummed, as if she'd heard that idea expressed before but still wasn't really convinced. Again, she got up; again, she went to the window and fiddled with its curtains. "I really shouldn't have come back, you know? Poor Ty just sounded so needy on the telephone. I always did have a soft spot for him—as you very well know." She glanced fully at her daughter and flashed an attractively youthful smile. "I suppose that's why I was so anxious for you two to get back together. Ty always seemed such a stable young man. An ideal husband for any woman in a world full of completely unsuitable young men."

Alyssa could have debated Ty's stability, considering his recent rampage of shooting bulls and authoring poison-pen letters, but she didn't.

"Why should you listen to your mother, or to anyone else, when making decisions of the heart? God knows, your mother certainly didn't pay too much attention to anyone, either. My, oh, my, though, didn't I make a mess of things in not doing so?"

"Were all your choices so bad?" Alyssa asked, eventually hoping to steer the conversation back to Ladonna Hidalgo.

"Oh, your father was certainly the best of the lot." Again, she moved the curtains and peered out as if she saw things which had occurred in the courtyard years ago when last she'd not only been in the hacienda but mistress of it. "He was fun, but thought there was more to marriage than just good times. He wanted to play father, and, for awhile, I was quite ready to let him. But, Lalo Montego? My God, that man was a walking time bomb for any women! He held nothing sacred, except possibly, at one time, his friendship for Joaquín Hidalgo."

"I thought you told me he botched even that."

"He was well on his way to doing just that, for sure," Karen admitted. "That was one of the main reasons I decided to leave him. I figured I didn't have much chance of keeping his loyalty when he seemed so hell-bent on shattering the one friendship he had left since his boyhood."

"Everyone I've spoken to, here, seems under the impression the two men remained friends up until Lalo died."

Karen turned back toward the bed and said, "Tell me, what exactly *you* have against Ladonna Hidalgo?" She folded her arms across breasts kept elevated by plastic surgery.

"It's a long story, mother," Alyssa said, "and, probably, in the final analysis, one based mainly on very little more than petty jealousy."

"Sometimes it does help to talk about these things, you know?" Karen said; a small smile was back on her lips.

"Touché, mother!" Alyssa finished off the rest of the orange, surprised at how quickly she was regaining her strength.

Once again, Karen came back to the bed and sat down on it. She reached for her daughter's hands and held them within her own.

"I must have looked horribly upset when Joaquín dropped his little bomb that you and Adriano Montego were 'interested' in each other. I kept imagining how my own daughter would soon be forced into undergoing the very same brutal nonsense that I'd endured with a Montego. I haven't been much of a mother to you, Alyssa, but I really do want you to be happy. Do you love him?"

"Actually, I have my doubts."

"What kind of doubts?"

Alyssa shrugged. Still, she resolved to try and put her feelings into words. Since she had always complained that her mother was never one for mother-daughter talks, she couldn't very well be faulted for trying one now—even if it appeared a little late in the day.

"Adriano was engaged to Ladonna...."

"What?" Karen interrupted, even though it was obvious Alyssa had been prepared to say more. "Adriano Montego and Ladonna Hidalgo? Engaged?"

"It's a logical marriage when you think about it, mother," Alyssa said. "Joaquín and Lalo were friends. They had adjoining ranches which could have been combined by the marriage."

"What a sick bastard Lalo had to have been to put his stamp of approval on that!" Karen said, screwing her face up in genuine disgust. She shut her eyes and physically shuddered.

"Actually, Adriano thought his father was really against it and that Lalo left the ranch to me so the wedding wouldn't go through. Though, Adriano, nor anyone else, seems to know why that might have been his plan."

"Well, *I* know!" Karen said, seeing finally why her daughter had ended up with the ranch that should have belonged to Adriano Montego. "I'm glad to discover that Lalo had a limit to his perversions, beyond which even he wasn't prepared to go."

"*You* know?" Alyssa pressed.

"They loved each other, did they? Adriano and Ladonna?" Karen ignored her daughter's query.

"Adriano says, no. He insists it was merely something they were prepared to do because Joaquín would have liked it to happen. Adriano doubts Ladonna can ever really love anyone."

"Like father, like daughter, "Karen said.

"You think Joaquín incapable of love?" Certainly, Alyssa was ready to give him the benefit of a doubt.

"Of course, *Joaquín* is capable of love." Karen gave Alyssa's hands a hearty squeeze. "He loved Elisa and Lalo Montego to a fault."

"Elisa?" Her mother had lost her.

"Joaquín's wife, my dear, back in those prehistoric days when your mother was mistress of this hacienda. Later, I heard she died when Ladonna was born. The wages of sin, and all of that, I supposed."

Alyssa waited for her mother to clarify, and Karen, after a preparatory sigh, did so. "Joaquín was in Madrid, arranging for the sale of some bulls, or whatever it is men do when they pack up and head off for days on end. Lalo took advantage and, as it turned out, Elisa wasn't all that adverse to his attentions."

"Ladonna is Lalo and Elisa's daughter?"

"Shall we sit, here, and count the months?"

CHAPTER EIGHT

It was time. Adriano knew it. Alyssa knew it. Yet, they both lingered a bit longer within the warmth offered by the covers and by each other's naked flesh.

"I have to go, babe," he said finally, giving her a kiss before pulling away.

She let him get up. She wouldn't hold him back; even though, she was filled with a definite apprehension regarding that afternoon he would spend in the *corrida* with six bulls.

"It's just something I have to do," he said. "Not for my dead father. Not for Fanuco. Not even for Sister Dominica's orphanage; although, that is probably as good a reason as any. I have to do it to prove something to myself. Prove that I *can* do it."

Alyssa thought the whole ritual came across as some kind of primitive initiation, like that of those African tribes who had to have its male members individually go forth and kill a lion with a spear before officially considered ushered into adulthood. If the notion was absurd that Adriano had to kill six bulls before he could become his own man, it was no more absurd than so many of life's other many foibles.

"I have to know," he said, "whether I kept out of the ring only to spite my father, or because I really didn't have the inclination or skill to be a matador. Up until now, I really don't have the answer, but I will after this afternoon."

Alyssa laid there in the bed, watching the man she loved. Simultaneously, she coveted the warmth his body had left in the bed with her.

He dressed, but not yet in the traditional suit of lights. He would don that later, along with the traditional *montera* and false *coleta*, within a small room at the *Plaza de Toros*. Then, after that, he would go to a small arena chapel and pray.

After he left her in their hotel room, the next time Alyssa would see him would be when he was entering the bullring, the heavy silk of his embroidery-encrusted costume catching brilliant rays of the afternoon sunshine. She was uneasy. She was afraid for him but she wouldn't try to stop him, intuitively knowing that the best way to hold onto a man was often just giving him leave to go.

It wasn't as if he was leaving her forever. No way! He was Lalo Montego's son, and how many fiestas had Lalo gone through before his moment of death in the afternoon? Even Lalo's eventual death on the horn of a bull became suspect, considering the incestuous marriage ceremony it aborted.

When Adriano finished dressing, he came over to the bed, leaned down, and kissed her again. She wrapped his neck with her arms, pulling him down closer. When he pulled away, this time, he said. "You will come?"

"I wouldn't miss it for the world."

"Good." He kissed her fingertips, hesitated a moment, and then left.

Alyssa checked her wristwatch. It was three o'clock. The bullfight was scheduled to begin promptly at six. *Six in the afternoon:* there was a poem that kept repeating that phrase over...and over...and over.

She had plenty of time. The hotel was within easy walking distance of the Plaza. Adriano had purposely booked them into a room that had assured their being together as long as possible.

She filled the tub with bath salts and hot water. She submerged herself into the steaming bubbles and liquid, and she shut her eyes.

Did she know what she was letting herself in for, falling in love with Adriano Montego? She really didn't have the answer to that—yet. She only knew that she did love him. She loved him with all of her heart and soul, and now she was quite positive he loved her. Certainly, he would have had to be an exceptional actor to have faked his passion of the night before.

"Surely, you need your rest," she had told him during one point in the course of their lovemaking. She had wanted him to know that she would have understood had he decided to forego passion for sleep.

"I never prescribed to the old wives' tale that sex drains a man of his strength," he had told her, his lips moving sensuously against her ear. "Quite to the contrary...."

She left the bathtub and dried. She dressed and checked herself out in the mirror. She was looking good! She was looking *very* good! Obviously, being in love agreed with her.

She tried to imagine how she would look, there in the bullring stands when Adriano dedicated his first bull to her, as he said he planned.

"The first bull should be dedicated to the woman I so love," he had told her.

What would Ladonna Hidalgo have to say to that? Probably very little. Ladonna seemed quite resolved to her upcoming role as wife to a man over three times her age. That she didn't love Victoro Isidro probably made little difference to her. She hadn't loved Adriano Montego, either, and she had been prepared to marry him.

Alyssa gave herself one more once-over. Then, she left the hotel room, locking the door behind her.

On the street, she was immediately caught up in the stream of people en route to Madrid's great bullring, the *Plaza Monumental*. She checked to make sure she had her ticket. Scalpers were getting even bigger fortunes for the small slips of red-and-yellow paper that gave access to the bullring that afternoon, since it had been revealed that it would be Adriano Montego, not Fanuco de Galena in the arena. It wasn't everyday the son of Lalo Montego took to the *corrida*—for charity, or for otherwise.

The whole atmosphere was one of charged excitement. Huge photographs of Adriano were plastered on almost every flat surface. Bullfight posters announced the fight in bright splotches of color that wrapped every pole.

Literally hundreds of people moved with Alyssa through the Moorish arches of the building. Hundreds more arrived via the two subway stations that flanked the front of the Plaza.

Cars, buses, and taxis were all involved in the massive traffic jam in the streets on all sides. Angry drivers honked horns that rose in loud cacophony.

Vendors hawked their wares: candies, chewing gum, soft drinks, lottery tickets, postcards....

Alyssa found the reserved box that already had Joaquín Hidalgo in it, waiting for her. Ladonna had excused herself to sit in the box her fiancé, Victoro

Isidro, had acquired for himself and several of his family and friends. Alyssa was glad Ladonna wouldn't be close. That woman's oddness made Alyssa uneasy, especially now that Alyssa knew Ladonna was Lalo Montego's daughter.

"Ah, Alyssa!" Joaquín exclaimed in greeting. "I just left Adriano a few moments ago. I must say, he's in exceptionally good spirits. And you, my dear, look radiant. Obviously, love is a wonderful stimulant, yes?"

"Yes," she agreed.

Joaquín's attention was diverted by one of the gentlemen in an adjoining box. After first introducing Alyssa, he became involved in an animated discussion with the man concerning the *muleta* style of *El Viti* compared to the cape work of the great Belmonte.

Alyssa was glad for the respite. She didn't feel like talking. What she wanted to do was sit there and soak up the ambience, like a sponge soaked up water. She needed time to realize she had fallen in love with a man who might yet become one of Spain's top matadors. Adriano was good; even Alyssa had seen that when he'd faced a mere heifer at the Hidalgo Hacienda.

In the Presidential Box, the Commissioner and his guests had taken their seats. At his disposal, he had four handkerchiefs: green to register a bad bull; red to request special *banderillas* for a specific animal; blue to honor the death of any exceptionally brave bull and have it dragged in a triumphant turn around the ring; white to award the matador's performance with a dead bull's ear, ears, and/or tail. The white would also begin the *corrida*.

The Commissioner laid the white handkerchief over the wooden balustrade in front of him. The trumpeter across the ring, waiting that very signal, put his musical instrument to his lips and began the first metallic notes in announcement of the beginning of *la fiesta brava*.

Alyssa came to her feet with the rest of those thousands in the stands with her.

The procession appeared from the shadow-clogged corridor that gave access to the sand of the arena.

Amid the strains of the band playing the traditional *pasodoble*, amid the deafening screams of the fans, Alyssa's heart thrilled at the sight of her lover's appearance into the blinding light of the afternoon sunshine.

ABOUT THE AUTHOR

WILLIAM MALTESE is a long-time wine connoisseur, and author (with Bonnie Clark) of the bestselling *Back of the Boat Gourmet Cooking*, and *Even Gourmands Have to Diet*, as well as (with Adrienne Z. Milligan) of the bestselling *The Gluten-Free Way: My Way*—both for the Borgo Press imprint of Wildside Press. He's traveled much of the world, drinking good wine and eating good food at each and every opportunity. He has finally decided to put down some of his thoughts on fine wining and dining for THE TRAVELING GOURMAND series books for Wildside Press. He's also been honored with a listing in the prestigious *Who's Who in America*. For more information on William, please check out his websites:

www.williammaltese.com
www.facebook.com/williammaltese
www.facebook.com/flickerwarriors
www.facebook.com/draqual
www.myspace.com/williammaltese
www.myspace.com/flickerwarriors
www.myspace.com/draqual
www.myspace.com/maltesecandlegallery

www.theglutenfreewaymyway.com
www.mxi.myvoffice.com/williammaltese (Xoçai®)

www.ingramcontent.com/pod-product-compliance
Lightning Source LLC
Chambersburg PA
CBHW050751250626
47155CB00005B/2014